THE UNEXPECTED MATCH

NOOR

Made with ♥ on the Notion Press Platform
www.notionpress.com

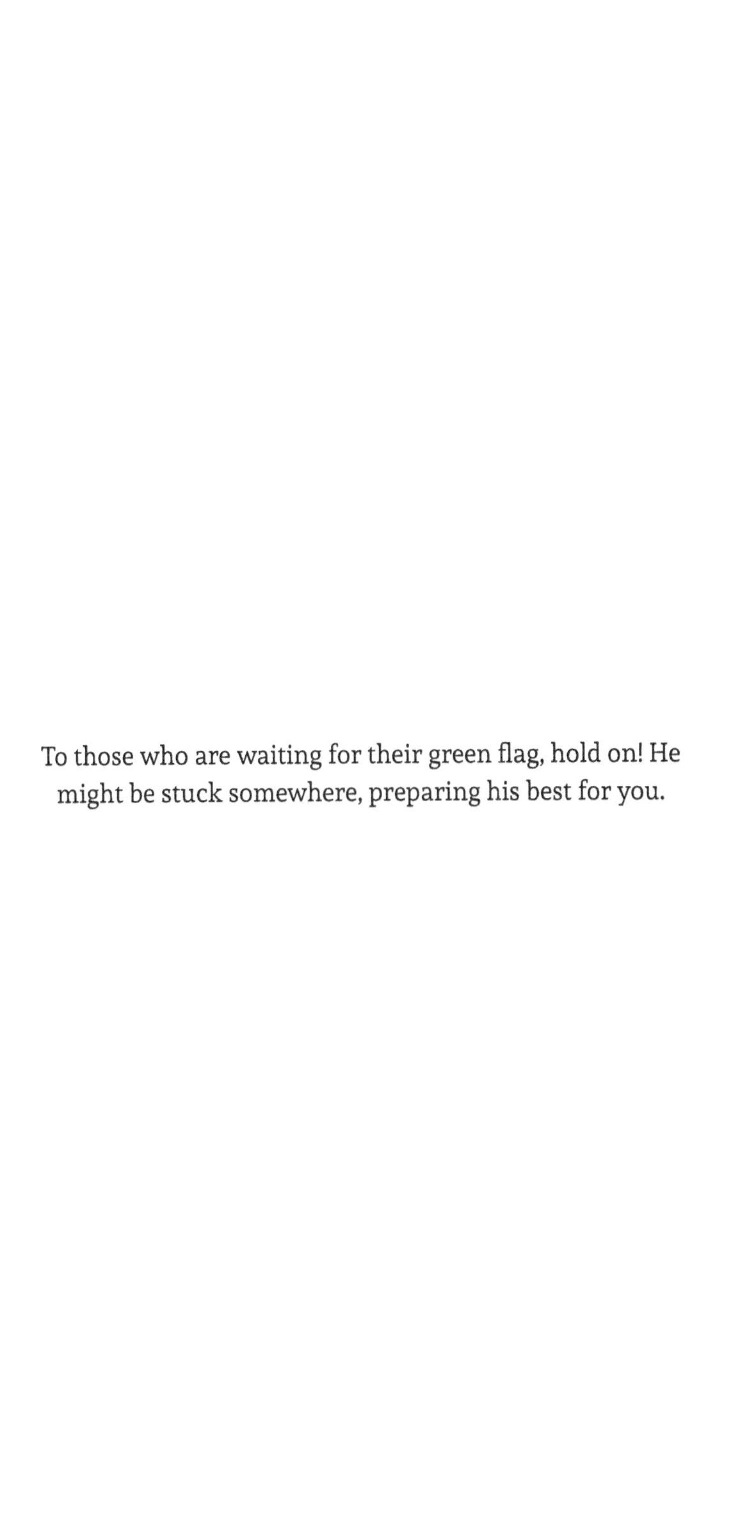

To those who are waiting for their green flag, hold on! He might be stuck somewhere, preparing his best for you.

Contents

Contents

Acknowledgements

First of all I want to thank my readers for all the incredible support, love, and motivation you've showered me with. I really mean it!

I want to thank my family, especially my mom. Mom, thank you for always encouraging me and for being my biggest supporter! I know you were even more excited than me to publish this book!

And I want to thank my amazing friends, especially Adina and Fari. Adina, I love love love the way you always motivate me. Thank you for standing by my side and constantly telling me that I can do it. And Fari, a huge thank you for stepping up as my editor and being there for me whenever I felt like I couldn't do it. I can't express how grateful I am to you!

Alhamdulillah for everything.

ONE
ALEENA

**December, 2018**

**Dhaka, Bangladesh**

The clock strikes nine, and I gaze at my jumbled room, filled with a chaotic array of my clothes. Shirts, pants, and dresses are scattered all over my room, making the whole space a complete mess. I've been trying on clothes for a solid two hours, but I still can't decide what to pack for my upcoming trip.

Picking out clothes is certainly the hardest thing I have ever done. One moment, I pick an outfit that seems perfect, but the next, I have doubts about it.

I often wonder if all women go through this, or if I am the weird one here.

Maybe.I.am.

As I debate between a denim jacket and a cozy sweater, my phone suddenly rings. Turning back, I glance at my phone screen, and soon my lips curl into a smile. Throwing off my clothes, I jump on my bed to grab my phone. "Hey, Sara!" I exclaim. "You don't have a clue about the wreck I'm in at this moment. I'm so muddled up and still can't figure out what to pack."

In the next moment, I can hear my best friend laughing on the other end of the line. "I can seriously picture your room right now. It must be a total disaster."

I chuckle, feeling instantly better.

"By the way, when are you planning to come? I already miss you!!" Sara asks.

I lazily swoop up a pillow placed next to me and plop it behind my back, against the headboard, to get all snuggled up in a cozy position. "We'll be catching the morning flight tomorrow from Dhaka to Chattogram. So, see you in less than twenty-four hours!"

"Ugh! I can't wait anymore" she exclaims, giving a little wiggle. I smile, before continuing again. "But seriously, girl, I'm so happy that you called. I really need your help right now."

"Always here for you. What's bothering my bestie?" Sara replies as she rests her chin on her palm and focuses on the screen.

"Let me show you," I switch the audio call to video to show her the mess I've created. Getting off my bed, I grab the purple kurti. "Look at this kurti," I say, holding it up for her appraisal. "Should I pair it with these baggy jeans or go with these salwar pants?"

She scrutinizes for a moment until she finally answers. "Hmm, I think jeans would be perfect."

"Alright! Now, take a look at these two kameezes," I continue, presenting the delicate peach-colored one and the elegant black one. "Which one should I go with?"

She chuckles in response. "Take both! Why not? You will look gorgeous in both!"

I let out a huge dramatic sigh, feeling a mix of amusement and indecision. "Stop Sara, you are making me even more confused now!"

She giggles once again. "Okay, show me more." Sara listens to me intently as I pour out my fashion perplexity, and after a short while, I finally manage to sort out half the mess.

"Okay! Check out these two lehengas, tell me which one looks best on me?" I ask, draping the lehenga over myself while with a swift turn of the camera, I make sure my bestie can have a proper view of it in the mirror.

"Alee! You look so gorgeous in both of these! To be honest, I'm more confused this time," she replies, which causes me to shake my head. "My suitcase has zero capacity to fit these two lehengas together, so you better help me choose one, Sara Zafar!"

"Alright! Let me observe."

It's been practically four years since Sara and I have been best friends. Well, online best friends. It's pretty wild how we were able to form such a strong bond, even though we didn't have the privilege to meet face to face due to being in different countries. What's even crazier is that for me, my friendship with Sara is stronger than any I've had before.

Our online chats and regular calls are like the thread that weaves us together. Sara and her family are US citizens, although they are originally from Bangladesh. Her upbringing and education have all been in the US.

But now, fate has given us the chance to bridge that distance. Within just three weeks, Sara's elder brother Sahil will be tying the knot. Although he's already done with his Akht, so technically he's married.

However, to honor their cultural traditions, Sara's family have decided to hold the other wedding ceremonies in Bangladesh. So here they are, staying in their house in Chattogram. It wasn't too long ago when I received the invitation to join the wedding. Sara demands that I show up two weeks before the wedding as she wants us to enjoy every second together.

After ending my call with Sara, I swiftly grab the clothes we have chosen together. I begin pushing them into my bag when, in a moment, the reverberating sound of the door opening up catches my attention.

In no time, my mom comes in. "Aleena, dear, come out for dinner. Your dad and I are waiting for you." Just as she glances around the room, she cups my forehead. "Ya Allah! Look at this girl! What have you done to your room?"

I flash a nervous smile while scratching the back of my neck. "Don't worry, Mom. I'll take care of it."

She sighs, wearing her usual 'Asian mom' frustrated articulation. "When will you learn to stay organized, Aleena?"

"I dunno, but for now, I'm super hungry," I answer and see a slight grin framing on her lips. "Come. We are waiting for you," she replies and swiftly exits my room. Pausing my packing, I grasp my phone in a swift motion and scamper out of my room.

With each step I take towards the dining room, the sight of my mom and dad comes into focus before me. "Dad, you're back from the office," I smile as I glance at my dad sitting on a chair. "Yes, my daughter, come sit with us." Nodding at him, I take a seat next to my mom.

"So, did you pack your bags?" my voice muffled as I'm invested in stuffing the food into my mouth. "I'm done packing, but your mom is still halfway through," my dad replies, as a laugh crawls up his throat, which earns me a smile. "How would you know!? We women need a lot of time to sort things out," my mom lets out a sigh.

I laugh. "Exactly! Even I was so confused, but then Sara called and that's it! She helped me, and now I'm done!

Honestly, I'm so excited!"

"So am I. It's been a long time since we attended a proper wedding. Plus, I can finally take a few days off from office work!" my dad says, with excitement in his voice.

"I agree!" my mom adds.

When it comes to my parents, they've always had my back. Whether it's because I'm the only child of my parents or other undisclosed factors, I always get the affection and backing I need in my life from them. I love them so much!

TWO

ALEENA

I return to my room to do the rest of the packing. I place the large suitcase full of clothes by the door and grab a smaller one for my accessories.

As I unzip the smaller suitcase, meant only for my precious accessories, a whole new kind of excitement surges through me. After all, it's one of my favorite phases of packing. I begin to place the accessories into the bag individually. Among them are a few western pieces that I've collected over the years. Yet, my heart also holds an exceptional spot for the Desi accessories that are going to give me a totally new look at the wedding.

I scoop up each item and gently arrange them within the confines of the suitcase. As I figure out that I'm all packed up, I swiftly close the lid of the smaller suitcase and take a deep breath.

I'm happy. I'm excited to experience this new journey.

Since my parents and I are taking the early morning flight, we have to wake up early to get prepped as soon as possible. But on the other hand, it's not an issue for us either, as we have to wake up for Fajr Salah anyway. I finish my prayer and stand up, gently creasing the prayer mat before settling it back in its place.

It's early morning, with the sun barely casting a soft orange glow across the sky. I have no craving to eat so early, so I skip it while my mom and dad insist I eat something, saying it's not good for my health. But I certainly don't want to throw up at this exciting moment.

However, I have a light breakfast on the plane because I don't want my parents to worry. The flight takes around 50 minutes, and as we disembark, I eagerly glance around the busy airport hoping to catch a glimpse of Sara. And shortly thereafter, my gaze stops at a familiar figure. Without a moment's delay, I bolt forward and jump over my best friend to embrace her with every last bit of my love.

"Sara!!! Oh my girl!! I missed you!" I exclaim, my arms enveloping my bestie in a firm squeeze. "I can't believe we finally met!"

"I feel ya girl!" Sara's voice vibrates against my body as her arms around me tightens.

"And look at you! You look prettier in person!" She adds, taking a step back, causing me to giggle. "Not more than you!" I reply, and I can hear my parents laughing from behind, gazing at me and Sara.

Glancing at my parents, Sara steps forward to greet them. And then she escorts us to her car.

Placing the suitcases, we all settle into the car.

"I'm finally here after so many months. It feels so good," I say, gazing out the window.

"And look at me. It's been years since I've been back! And let me tell you, the happiness of returning to your homeland can't be expressed in words!" Sara exclaims, prompting me to nod in agreement. "I agree!"

"You know what's crazy? Even though I'm back in my homeland, it's like I'm seeing the city with fresh eyes. Everything feels so new and different. A lot has changed and developed since I was last here."

"No worries, bestie, I'm here for you. Although I'm from Dhaka, I know all about Chattogram too. So, if there's anywhere you want to go, I'll be your aide! Just depend on me!" I answer, blazing a wide grin.

The whole ride is far from silence as Sara and I eagerly spill all the stories we've been keeping to ourselves. Amidst our conversation, my parents burst out laughing, thoroughly enjoying our barely comprehensible crackhead discussions.

After reaching Sara's home, we all descend the car and head inside. As my eyes gaze ahead of me, I notice a huge modern house. The sunlight pours over the tall structure with those large windows, making them all shiny and bright. Moreover, the clean lines and modern architecture give the house a sophisticated and stylish look. There is a huge lawn that's busy with rich green grass, and there is a line of flowers adding to the beauty of the lawn. Plus, there are some round tables and chairs, as well as a comfy bench, where a person can just chill and have a great time.

"Why are you still standing here? Let's go inside first, then I'll bring you back here," Sara's abrupt voice hauls me out of my thoughts as I feel her grip around my wrist. As we step inside, Sara's awesome parents and some family members who happen to be her cousins and aunts, give us the warmest welcome ever!

I greet them, and as I had anticipated, Sara's parents are incredibly best, particularly her mom.

"Lets go, I'll take you to my room" Sara practically yanks me upstairs to her room while her mother is occupied with showing my parents the room she has arranged for them. I step inside and cast my eyes around the gigantic room, which is perfectly adorned; nevertheless, I can't ignore the mess my bestie has created on her bed with a few clothes and accessories. After all, it's wedding season!

Grabbing both of my wrists, Sara giggles. "I can't believe this is really happening! Finally you're here!"

I chuckle. "You seem more excited than me."

"Of course I am! Oh, by the way, I've got a surprise for you!" She says, pulling me towards her dressing table and opening the top drawer.

My eyes widen as I see her taking out two pairs of matching yellow-decorated jhumkas. "Sara! They are so pretty!"

"They had to be! I specially bought these for you and me. We're gonna wear these for the Holud ceremony."

"Awww, Sara, this is so cute!" I admire the pair of jhumkas briefly before setting them back. And then I stroll over to the window to peer out over the grass once more.

"Love at first sight, I see," Sara's sudden voice casts a shadow of confusion on my face.

"Huh?" I ask.

"You fell in love with the lawn ever since you saw it; I've noticed it. It was pretty obvious after all."

A chuckle creeps up my throat as I hear my best friend. "You can read me so well, huh?"

"I'm a psychology student, after all," She replies, and we burst out laughing.

"Since you found out about my first love, then why don't you take me to my love?"

"I couldn't want anything more than to make it happen. We should go, best friend." she answers, attempting to keep a similar sensational expression as me, which earns me another chuckle.

Together we make our way downstairs. "Here you go, bestie! Take your love!" Sara says dramatically, wiping her imaginary tears. I giggle and look around, admiring each and everything which gives me a sort of peace.

I get so caught up in admiring my surroundings that I don't realize there's someone behind me. I end up accidentally bumping into him, causing his phone to drop. Turning around, I grab the phone and stand back with a sudden guilt wracking my whole body. "I'm sorry! I'm really sorr-" I stop, unable to complete my words as my eyes choose the individual before me.

My heart skips a beat as I realize who is standing right in front of me. Tall figure, wearing gray sweats, paired with a hoodie and white shoes. I move my eyes away from him, feeling something inside me.

"Oh! Aleena, let me introduce my other brother, Samir!" Sara says, dragging me out of my own thoughts. As I look back at him, I find his eyes waiting on me, expecting me to utter something. I pause for a moment, trying my best to gather myself and voice the words that are caught in my throat. "Umm... Hi."

He smiles. "Hello, Ms.?"

My breath hitches.

"Uh, Aleena, it's Aleena," I answer, my eyes fixated on the dimples on his cheeks.

I find myself not able to look directly into his eyes nor speak properly before him, which apparently never happened before in my life. A social butterfly like me can't express even a single word before him, and I have no idea what's going on inside me.

"That's a pretty name," his sudden voice makes me look back at him again.

As he looks at Sara, who is remaining close to me, he ruffles her hair gently. "I'm taking a walk and will eat out. If Sahil Bhaiya wakes up, tell him to call me. I've something important to talk about with him."

"Okay, Bhaiya, don't worry," Sara replies with warmth occupying her smile. "Alright then. I'm taking my leave," he says and settles his eyes once again on me, forming a slight smile on his lips. "Bye."

I freeze in my spot.

Because I'M WEAK FOR DIMPLES!

Somehow suppressing the nervousness inside me, I grin back.

Waving at us, he makes his way out. I let my eyes linger on his departing figure until he disappears out of my sight.

He is considerably more handsome than the photos I have seen of him on Sara's social media. Truly, I have had eyes for him ever since, yet it was never love, perhaps it wasn't liking on the other hand. But I never, ever expected that his presence would have such a profound impact on me in that very moment.

THREE
SAMIR

I grab my watch and wrap it around my wrist before looking at myself through the mirror one final time.

It's another beautiful morning in Chattogram. The colder time of year is practically here, although I, a man who has lived most of my life in the US, am not precisely impacted by the cold here. The temperature barely drops to 17 degrees in the morning, and even that is nothing to me.

I have a plan to take a walk and taste a few delicious customary Bengali breakfasts from the nearby places. Having lived most of my life with western culture, I miss my own culture a lot. Despite the fact that there are many spots in the US where I can track down Bengali food varieties, as far as I'm concerned, nobody can make the best ones like the Bengalis themselves.

I grasp my phone from the bed and review the places I plan to go. At that very moment, my mom comes in, causing me to look over at her. "Mom?"

"Samir, you're going somewhere?" she asks as she takes a once-over at me.

"Mom, seriously? I just told you a little while ago," I say, gazing at my mother while shaking my head. She pauses for a moment, presumably attempting to think about what I'm referring to until it finally hits her. "Oh! I remembered now. The way I'm failing to remember everything. I don't know when I'll forget my own name."

This time, we both laugh.

"By the way, I came to ask if you are available tomorrow," she inquires.

"Tell me if there's anything. Even if I'm not available, I'll still make sure to get your work done," I answer, causing a smile to shape her lips.

"Actually, we haven't yet bought the gifts we planned to give the members of the bride's family. Your chachi and I will handle the shopping for the female members. Yet, about the males, I don't think I can choose properly. Besides, your father busy with other things. So, get the gift shopping done by tomorrow. Ask your brother to join you so you can both choose together."

I nod immediately. "Don't worry, Mom. I'll take care of it."

I watch my mom let out a sigh of relief. "All set then. Likewise, I didn't discuss it with Sahil yet. I went to his room, but he was still sleeping. Talk to him once he wakes up and make the timetable when you both are going."

"As you order, Mom," I answer, causing my mom to giggle. "Okay, I have to go. We have new guests, so I'll look at them."

I frown. "Guests? Who?"

"Aleena and her parents," she answers. This time confusion clouds over me considerably more as I somehow feel the name is familiar, yet I can't exactly recall where I heard it.

At last, realization dawns upon me. "Isn't she the one Sara talks about all the time?"

My mom grins. "Yes, she is the one. Sara's best friend."

"They should be currently at the lawn, as I saw them going out while I was coming to you," she adds, making me glance down through my window right away.

I spot this lady, Aleena, grabbing Sara and pulling her to the center of the lawn, and in the following second, the two of them burst into laughter together. Although I am unable to hear what they are talking about, I can see it's a funny or, most likely, an irrational discussion of some sort.

"I'm going," I hear my mother from behind, and soon I no longer feel her presence in my room. However, my eyes are still down, observing my sister's best friend.

She's busy giggling with Sara, and in the next moment, her face turns in my direction, allowing me to see her face properly and for the first time. I smile and I don't have any idea why.

But just as realization dawns upon me, I promptly tear my eyes away and shake off my thoughts. I leave my room and head out. But out of nowhere, someone straight up bumps into me, and my phone slips right out of my hand. I turn around, and notice Aleena.

This time she turns around, looking completely guilty. "I'm sorry! I'm really sorr-" She can't finish her words as her eyes settle on me. I see her looking away for a moment, but then our eyes meet again.

I remain quiet, waiting for her to initiate the conversation. My eyes are drawn to her cheeks that are forming a blood-red shade, making her look even prettier, but I do whatever it takes not to look, knowing that if I do, I won't be able to take my eyes off her.

"Umm... Hi," she says.

I hear her velvety voice and feel an unexpected warmth possessing my chest. Yet I manage to stay normal with a simple smile. "Hello, Ms.?" I ask. Even though I already know her name, all I want is to hear her voice again.

And I'm not understanding what I'm truly doing.

"Uh, Aleena, it's Aleena," she answers.

I smile. "That's a pretty name."

But just as my eyes drop on Sara, I reach out to gently ruffle her hair. "I'm taking a walk and will eat out. If Sahil Bhaiya wakes up, tell him to call me. I've something important to talk about with him."

"Okay Bhaiya, don't worry," she replies with a smile. "Alright then. I'm taking my leave," I say and settle my eyes once again on Aleena.

A part of me waits for her to say something, but somehow I pull it together while shaping a slight grin on my lips. "Bye."

And she smiles back.

FOUR
ALEENA

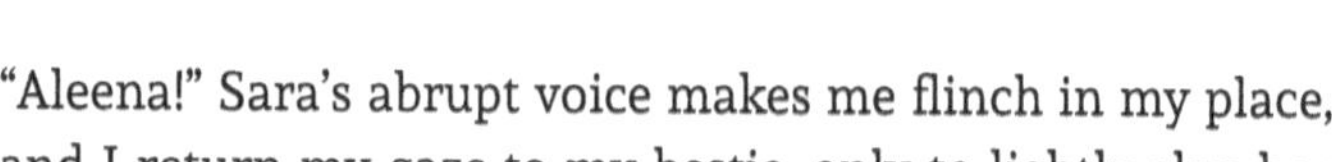

"Aleena!" Sara's abrupt voice makes me flinch in my place, and I return my gaze to my bestie, only to lightly slap her arm. "You scared me!"

"That's what I wanted," she says, her voice slurring between laughter.

"Jokes apart, you must be tired. Let's go to my room, you can take a nap,"

I chuckle. "Honestly, I need it right now. Let's go!"

We walk into the house and are about to go upstairs when Sara's mom intercepts us, a concerned look on her face. "Aleena, dear, you haven't eaten anything since you came here. You must be starving!"

I grin. "Thank you, Aunty, but I'm really not hungry right now. You don't need to worry about me."

"Darling, you're our guest. How can we let you not eat anything? It won't look good. Come on, join us for a quick bite. Your parents are waiting for you too."

I smile, knowing I can't resist her convincing powers any more. With a nod, I join them at the breakfast table.

♡

As my eyes ripple open from my sleep, I extend my arms and let out a yawn. Reaching for my phone, I check the time and realize I've been snoozing for roughly two hours. Turning back, I notice Sara fixing some of her clothes that are messed up on her couch.

"What are you doing?" I ask, even though I can see what my best friend is up to I just want to begin a conversation. "Oh, you woke up. I was fixing the mess I've created here. If Mom sees these, she will kill me!"

I laugh at her answer. "I can relate to you. Moms can't see our rooms messy."

Turning back, I reach for a hair clip and swiftly secure it around my hair. Grabbing my phone, I sit back on the edge of the bed while I sense Sara walking towards the bathroom. "I'll be right back," she says, and I reply with a simple nod.

Abruptly I hear a knock on the door, and in the next moment, the door is wide open, revealing Samir. I freeze in my place, not able to understand what to do, even though it isn't a situation to worry about.

As his eyes drop on me, his stride comes to an abrupt halt. "I'm sorry! I thought Sara was here!" He tries to be as polite as he can.

I streak an awkward smile. "It's alright. You don't need to say sorry. After all, it's your sister's room." I pause and continue again. "And Sara is in the bathroom, she will be right back. If you want, you can wait here."

His eyebrows raise silently, inquiring whether I'm certain, and I nod right away. I notice his body relaxing at my answer as he leans against the dressing table, which is directly opposite me as I'm sitting on the bed.

I observe his clothes. He has already changed them into a white shirt and black jeans.

And He Looks Breathtaking!

I return my eyes to my phone, unable to strike up a conversation with him.

"So, is this your first time in Chattogram?" he asks, certainly trying to ease the situation between us. "Uh, no. I've been here a few times before," I reply briefly, yet unable to lock my gaze with his.

"Are you generally this quiet?" He throws another question at me.

"She isn't at all. She never was. Maybe the main reason is you. She just turns out to be quiet before you. My bestie is scared of you, bhaiya." Sara's abrupt voice draws our attention to her.

I laugh awkwardly and then I shoot Sara a glare, which ends up making her laugh.

"Nah, it's not like that at all. She's just joking"

"I'm not joking. Not at all. I'm spilling the truth. Bhaiya, seriously, Aleena is scared of you."

"Is that so?" he asks.

As I return my gaze back to Samir, I notice him stepping toward me. Placing my hands on either side of the bed, I intuitively move back, yet he keeps on progressing.

Goosebumps take over my entire body as I catch a whiff of his intoxicating cologne. My breath catches in my chest as he leans nearer to my face, making me move back significantly further.

He moves his face from side to side.

"Do I really look scary?" he teases.

At that point, all my fantasies crumble.

No... You are the most breathtakingly gorgeous man I've ever seen. The words ring in my heart, urging me to express them in front of him. Nonetheless, I don't let my heart embarrass myself in front of him.

"I've already told you, Sara is joking," I quickly reply, feeling nervous and slightly embarrassed.

"Bhaiya, you will seriously scare her now,"

He looks at Sara, then back at me, and then he moves away from me.

"Anyways, I came here to get my AirPods. You took them from me last night," Samir says.

Sara sits there, attempting to unwind her hair from the brush. When her gaze meets her brother's, she casts him a pleading, puppy-eyed look, silently beseeching his aid. "When will you learn to fix your own hair? And why did you even grow your hair so long if you don't have the slightest idea how to deal with it?" Samir asks, shaking his head ever so slightly.

"Okay, sorry bhaiya. Now, please help me," Sara requests. Soon, I observe him walking over to her. Gently taking the comb from her hand, he begins carefully untangling her hair.

I gaze at him, observing his love and care for his sister. He knows how to prioritize relationships and fulfill his responsibilities in life. And that's somehow makes me drawn to him even more.

I don't realize I'm smiling at him until Sara speaks up. "Alee, why are you smiling?"

Samir's eyes land on me as silence takes over the room. He arches his brows, signaling me to speak, which I brush off with an awkward grin. "I, uh… Nothing. I should go check up on my parents real quick."

I hurriedly leave the room and feel my cheeks burning with sudden embarrassment. "What are you doing, Aleena?" I mumble to myself while descending the stairs.

My eyes widen when I glance down at the whole house filled with people, busy preparing for the wedding. The house is alive with activity and the delightful aroma of food. It's hard to believe how much the atmosphere has transformed since I arrived this morning. It had been quiet at that time, but now the house is bustling with energy and excitement.

As I pass through the drawing room, I suddenly spot my parents, who are immersed in discussion with Sara's parents and other family members. My lips shape into a smile.

All of a sudden, Sara appears before me, catching my attention. "You are already done with your hair?" I ask. "Yes. Anyways, come with me! I want you to meet my older brother, Sahil," she exclaims.

We stroll through the busy group, the vibrant decorations, and finally reach Sahil. He stands tall, a warm smile on his face. "Bhaiya! Meet my bestie Aleena. And Aleena, this is Mr. Groom," Sara introduces.

"Hey, Aleena! Finally, we get to meet," Sahil says.

I grin. "It's great to finally meet you too, Sahil bhaiya. And congratulations."

He chuckles. "Well, Sara told us a lot about you. And thank you for coming here to my wedding."

We continue the conversation, encompassed by the hustle and bustle of wedding preparations. At this moment, I realize how happy I am. It feels like ages since I have felt this much excitement and bliss in my life.

FIVE
ALEENA

"Do you think this will look good on me?" Sara asks, dangling a kameez over her, being completely indecisive. I stand before her, appeasing her from head to toe until finally, I decide to voice my answer. "Ummm, not sure. Let's check out others."

As we walk around the mall, I point out different stores and suggest clothes that would look good on Sara.

Sara hasn't done her shopping completely for her brother's wedding yet. Moreover, she wanted to spend some time exploring the city. That's when I suggest joining her. We left the house shortly after breakfast and spent the rest of the morning exploring some famous places in Chattogram until we ended up at the mall.

I'm not entirely certain if it's just us or if it's typical of others to feel torn between several options when choosing our own clothes. But in any case, when it comes to picking clothes for one another, we have an uncanny capacity to give the absolute best ideas.

Soon Sara ends up with a pile of clothes to try on. "Trust me, my young lady, based on my great fashion sense, these clothes I chose for you will make you look so pretty!" I exclaim, making my bestie laugh.

"And if these don't look good on me, you are going to pay!"

"Wait, what's that rule? I ain't payin'!"

"You are!"

After we wrap up our shopping binge, we choose to indulge ourselves with some delicious ice creams before we leave the mall. So we head to the food court and grab two ice creams.

"You Should've tried this chocolate flavor, it's so delicious," Sara says, savoring a spoonful Ice-cream. "That's bitter. I'm good with this Vanilla one," I reply, causing Sara to chuckle. "That's what actual dark chocolate tastes like. And that's the best thing about this ice cream."

I scoop up a spoonful of ice cream and shove it into my mouth. "Sara, don't eat too much bitter stuff. I'm apprehensive you'll turn out to be bitter too." In the next moment, both of us burst into laughter.

"Munching on ice cream in this cold weather?"

I exchange a glance with Sara before returning my attention to the owner of that familiar voice.

It's Samir, standing right in front of me.

I feel a gentle tug on my chest.

He is here.

He steals a quick glance at his sister before returning to me. I just stand there, unsure of how to react, my grip on the shopping bag straps growing tighter with each passing moment. On top of that, I can't deny the intensity in his eyes that is numbing me from within.

"What are you doing here bhaiya?" Sara asks, causing Samir to look back at her. "I was here for the gifts mom asked me to buy."

"And you shouldn't eat Ice cream now. It's cold out there," he adds, and soon glances back at me. "Same goes for you."

This time, I don't let those odd sentiments overwhelm me and cause me to feel embarrassed in front of him. "Well, we don't get snow around here, so I guess we'll be fine," I counter, flashing a cheeky smile.

His eyes flicker between the two of us for a moment and soon I can discover a smile on his lips, showing his adorable dimples. "Alright. Are you done shopping?" he asks.

"Yes bhaiya, we're all done," Sara replies. "Now we have to head back home," she adds.

"I'm done with my work too. Then let's go back home," he says.

I notice a bunch of girls checking him out from afar, but he couldn't care less about what's happening around him.

He's dangerously loyal to his future wife!

Once we exit the mall, Sara tugs at my arm to join me in the back seat. Just as she's about to climb in, she halts abruptly upon hearing Samir's voice. "I'm quite certain I don't look like your driver, do I?" His words infuse with a hint of wit as his eyebrows arch playfully at his sister.

Sara exhales slowly as her gaze briefly meets mine before shifting back to her brother, who observes her with a nonchalant expression, as if he's entirely accustomed to the eye roll she's giving him, delivered in the most polite manner possible. "Fine, I'll sit. No need to give me that look that sometimes makes me feel like you're being annoying even though you're really not. Just be the good, caring brother you really are," she replies, settling into the front seat.

I can't help but stifle a chuckle at their banter.

As I'm about to hop into the car, out of nowhere a man on a bicycle crashes into me, throwing me off balance. But luckily, I manage to recover quickly and stand back up on my feet.

"Hey, are you alright?" As I turn back, I see Samir has his arms encircling slightly away from me, and I realize that even if I did lose my balance completely, he could not have possibly let me fall.

"Please watch where you're going, sir! You could have injured her," He nearly shouts at the man, who quickly turns to me, offering an apologetic glance. "I'm so sorry!" he voices, barely finishing his words before hastily leaving.

Samir's gaze swiftly returns to me, transitioning from a scowl at the man to a look of concern. Before he has the chance to articulate the question I know is coming, I respond preemptively. "It's okay. I'm okay."

He falls silent, a gentle sigh escaping his lips as he diverts his gaze from me to the direction where the man has vanished, now beyond our sight, and then turns his attention back to me. The concern still lingers in his eyes. Yet, he holds back from asking anything further.

"Aleena, are you okay?" Sara asks, getting out of the car right away. "I'm fine, Sara. Don't worry," I reassure, smiling at my best friend. "Leave it. Let's go," I add and look back at Samir. "Let's go."

His concerned eyes remain fixed on me for a couple of seconds, and then he finally nods and gets into the car.

There has been a prolonged silence hanging in the car since we began our drive. Sara is comfortably settled next to Samir in the front seat, almost drifting off, which only amplifies the awkwardness for me, knowing that the only other presence in the car besides her is her brother.

"Aleena, are you sure you're okay?"

I nearly flinch at the sound of Sara's voice, which I had assumed was lost to sleep. She turns to me, concern etched across her features. But at the same time, I feel a wave of relief wash over me. At least I no longer have to bear the weight of this awkward silence.

I catch a fleeting glimpse of Samir's gaze through the rearview mirror, as if he, too, is waiting for my response, mirroring the concern of his sister. But then, he swiftly redirects his attention back to the road ahead.

"I'm completely fine, don't worry," I assure Sara, aware that he can hear me as well. The rest of the ride unfolds in complete silence until we arrive at their house. As we get out of the car, I reach for the shopping bags to assist Sara when Samir intervenes,"I'll take care of those. You both can relax."

"Have I ever told you just how much I love you, Bhaiya?" Sara glances at her brother, her face adopting a theatrical expression that elicits a soft chuckle from him. "Yes, countless times. Now, really, there's no need to butter me up any further."

Sara nonchalantly shrugs her shoulders. "If you think my love for you is just buttering up, then there's nothing I can do. Anyway, thank you for lugging the bags," she says, flashing an adorable smile before turning to head into the house. With a smile directed at her, I trail after her, only to be interrupted by the sound of my name being called from behind.

I come to a halt and swivel around, noticing Samir quickening his approach until he finally stands directly before me. I direct a curious gaze his way as he extends a small plastic bag toward me. "Make sure to apply the ointment before it has a chance to get infected," he urges.

My gaze follows his, landing on my wrist, where I finally notice a scrape I hadn't realized was there—likely the result of being brushed by the bicycle earlier in front of the mall.

To be honest, It's frustrating how those fluttering, delicate feelings emerge unbidden at his every little action, just like right now, when he noticed the scrape on my wrist—something I hadn't even acknowledged initially. I find it challenging to stay composed whenever he's around, as each encounter turns into an awkward struggle with emotions I'm not quite ready to accept, despite the undeniable warmth they bring.

"I'm fine, it's just a tiny scrape," I somehow manage to muster a faint smile, even though my lips are practically striving to consume my entire face.

Yet he doesn't seem convinced by my words as I watch him bring the bag closer, still waiting for me to accept it "That doesn't mean you can brush it off. Even the smallest injuries can lead to something serious"

Just as these subtle actions of yours are leading to something profound within my heart?

I reach out, accepting the bag into my hands. "Thank you."

This time, his cheeks light up with dimples. "No worries. You are my sister's best friend. It's our responsibility to ensure you don't face any issues here."

My smile vanishes. An odd discomfort envelops my chest, almost rendering it challenging to articulate any response, and it becomes even more disconcerting to realize how utterly absurd it is to feel this way when he himself isn't at fault. I am, after all, just his sister's best friend, and he sees me as such.

Lingering here any longer and allowing him to catch even the faintest glimpse of the chaotic emotions swirling within me would undoubtedly be the most embarrassing thing imaginable. So, I manage a quick "Thanks again" before swiftly turning away and walking off, just to escape his sight as swiftly as possible.

♡

I let out a yawn and glance at the laptop screen, leaning slightly against Sara's shoulder. "When will this end?" I ask, shifting my gaze between Sara and the movie playing on the screen. "My lady, we still got a whole hour left. This is the most thrilling part, and I don't wanna miss any of the clues. So, shh!"

My best friend is so into the story that she doesn't even turn her head, and it's clear that the movie has her completely hooked.

"But I'm starving!" I exclaim, a sigh escaping my lips. "You know where I stashed the snacks, just grab them and chow down," Sara replies. I shake my head. "Nah, I don't feel like eating those. Let's go to the kitchen instead," I offer, a wide smile spreading across my face, hoping she will agree. This time, Sara pauses the movie and turns to face me, with a pure 'I'm done' look. "It's 12:30 AM, girl."

"So what? There's a whole kitchen downstairs, and I'm sure we can find something edible there. Right?"

"Well, who's stopping you? Go on. Everything's up for grabs. Now let me get back to my movie," She says, returning her attention back to the screen.

I reach out and grab my best friend's arm. "It's your house, not mine. I feel awkward going to the kitchen alone. Please come with me."

"You won't find a single soul in the kitchen now. Everyone is sleeping. So feel free to go," She responds, her attention still fixed on the movie.

"You can just pause the movie and join me for a little while!"

But she just shakes her head. "Nah nah! I'm so curious at this moment. I don't wanna pause it."

I pick up my pillow and throw it at her face, hoping to grab her attention. But, she catches the pillow and remains focused on the movie, not even flinching. I sigh, realizing that I will have to go to the kitchen alone.

With slow and quiet steps, I make my way downstairs.

As I enter the kitchen, my eyes scan the room, searching for any sign of delicious food. I head towards the fridge, open it, and carefully examine it.

After a thorough search, a sigh escapes my lips because nothing seems interesting enough to satisfy my hunger. However, I decide to give the fridge one more look. And there it is, nestled among the other items—apples. With a swift motion, I grab an apple, close the fridge, and take a big bite.

But something is missing.

The hunger still lingers, and I let out another sigh. "Why do I have to feel so hungry today!"

Feeling a bit down, I turn around to make my exit. However, my motion comes to an abrupt halt as my gaze meets Samir's figure standing right before me.

"What are you doing here?" Both of us blurt out at the same time.

Silence hangs in the air as we await each other's response.

"I was just here to grab a drink of water. And you?" he asks.

I stand there, my hands instinctively retreating behind my back, unsure of my own actions.

His head tilts slightly, his eyes catching sight of the apple nestled in my grasp. "Uh, so someone's been stealing apples from here, huh?" He jests.

I bring my hand forward, revealing the apple. "Well, I was starving, and this apple was the only thing worth 'stealing' around here," I quip.

As my words reach his ears, he briefly avert his gaze, and I can see dimples forming on his cheeks.

He walks past me, smoothly reaching for the kitchen cabinet, retrieving a packet of pasta. I turn around, my eyes glued to his every move. "I had absolutely no idea that it was there!"

He flashes me a cheeky smile. "Well, maybe you should consider wearing glasses."

"I don't need glasses. I can even clearly see your dimples from here," I blurt out, my words trailing off as I realize what I've said. Catching my gaze, he places the packet on the kitchen island and leans against it, folding his arms. "So, you've been noticing my dimples too, huh?"

I glance away, my eyes wandering aimlessly for a moment before settling back on him. "It's noticeable enough for anyone."

He gathers the remaining ingredients from the fridge, and gets ready to start cooking. Curiously, I step closer and stand next to him, not too close but not too far either. He rolls up his sleeves and skillfully begins chopping the vegetables for the pasta. He places each ingredient onto the sizzling pan, moving them around with a wooden spoon and flipping them effortlessly.

And he looks absolutely gorgeous!

He carefully plates the pasta and holds it out to me. "There you go, it's done."

I glance down at the plate of pasta, then back up at him, and once again at the pasta. Swiftly taking the plate, I make my way to the small table tucked away in the corner of the kitchen. "Why didn't you take some for yourself?"

He grabs a tissue, wipes his hands, and tosses it into the small trash bin. "I'm not hungry. You can have it all."

I scoop up a spoonful of the pasta, savoring its mouthwatering aroma before bringing it to my lips. I chew, swallow, and close my eyes. "This is absolutely delicious!" I exclaim, my eyes still shut.

He smiles. "I'm relieved."

I take another spoonful of pasta and shove it into my mouth. "Like, how are you so good at cooking?"

"Well, I'm not an expert or anything, but I know a few dishes, including pasta," he walks back to me and places the tissue box in front of me. "Whenever I get hungry at odd times, pasta is my go-to."

He positions himself right in front of me. The small round table has just a few chairs around it.

With every bite I take, a broad smile lights up my face.

SIX
SAMIR

I plop my arms on the table and watch Aleena dig into the pasta. Honestly, I have no idea what I'm doing. I was here to drink water, and ended up making pasta just to see that smile on her face. She chows down, sneaks glances at me, and talks non-stop.

She.is.adorable.

I smile.

My gaze shifts downward, noticing a small trace of sauce lingering at the corner of her lips. I reach for a tissue and lean in closer, almost brushing her lips. But then I pause abruptly, realizing the potential awkwardness of my action.

Aleena pauses mid-chew and looks at me, puzzled. "Um, there's a tiny bit of sauce on your lips," my voice slightly trembles.

I hold out the tissue, silently offering her a way to clean it off.

She quickly grabs the tissue from my hand, wiping her lips. "Thanks for the pasta. I better head back. Sara's waiting for me," she mumbles, avoiding eye contact.

Jumping off the chair, she rushes to the sink, hastily washing her plate. I stand there, puzzled, observing her and grappling with the unresolved emotions I'm still feeling. Without giving me a chance to speak, she bolts out of the kitchen, disappearing from my view.

♡

The next day rolls around, and here I am, leaning against my car, waiting for my sister. Our mom had entrusted us with a special task – to purchase some items for the wedding. I lift my hand to check the time, and it's already eleven thirty in the morning. However, there's no sign of her yet.

I pull out my phone and about to call her when a familiar figure catches my eye, running towards me. "Aleena?"

She stands before me, catching her breath after that crazy sprint. It takes a few moments for her to regain composure, her gaze finally meeting mine. "I was supposed to come with Sara, but she's still sleeping. I tried to wake her up, but she insisted she was too tired. So, I had to come alone. But don't worry, I made sure to bring the list Auntie gave us."

I raise my eyes, observing her as she blurts out words in one breath, as if she's explaining something really serious.

She.is.adorable.

"Alrighty then, let's hop in the car," I say, swinging the door open of the passenger seat and giving her a quick glance. She looks at the seat, then at me, and then back at the seat again. With a slight nod, she strolls over and plops herself down. I close the door and make my way to the driver's seat, before settling in myself.

The car ride stretches on in complete silence, not a single word passing between us. I steal a few glances her way, hoping she'll catch me and initiate a conversation. But she remains silent, her gaze fixed outside the window.

The silence becomes almost unbearable, prompting me to break it finally. "Where should we head first?"

This time, she turns her gaze back to me, her hand reaching into her bag to retrieve her phone. With a few taps on the screen, she takes a quick look and then directs her attention back to me. "We have to get the dalas first," she says.

Once we arrive at the destination, we step out of the car and make our way into the shop. As we walk in, our eyes scans the vibrant dalas on display. A dala is basically a bamboo or cane basket that is intricately decorated and used to showcase the gifts for the bride and groom.

I stand there quietly, watching Aleena as she carefully examines each dala, running her fingers over the designs.

There's something about her presence that keeps me glued, unable to look away. We may not be super close, but there's something about her that draws me in, making everything feel so special. I can't quite put into words why I'm so engrossed in watching her, but one thing's for sure – she is too pretty to look away.

But then, a sudden realization hits me and I immediately lower my gaze. What are you doing, Samir? Stop staring at her! I mentally shout at myself, feeling a wave of guilt wash over me.

She is my sister's best friend!

What am I even thinking!?

This is the first time I've ever felt this way, and I hate to admit just how strongly I'm attracted to her.

As she continues to choose the dalas, I try really hard not to steal even a single glance at her. I shift my attention to anything else in the store, doing my best to distract myself from these forbidden feelings. Finally, she finishes making her selection, and we make our way back to the car.

I carefully place the packets in the trunk, trying to occupy my mind with the task at hand. Once everything is settled, I take a seat in the car. "So, where to next?" I ask.

She flips her phone screen to me. "This place"

And I drive to our destination.

After we wrap up our shopping, we walk back to the car and I try to fit all the bags into the trunk of the car, but there's just not enough space. I end up squeezing some of them onto the back seat, hoping they won't topple over. With everything settled, I turn around, expecting to find Aleena right there, but she just disappears. I take a look inside the car, but she's not there either. My heart starts racing as I frantically search through the bustling crowd, calling out her name. But I don't get any response. That's when I reach into my pocket and whip out my phone, ready to dial her number and figure out where she's gone off to. But then, a sudden realization hits me - I don't even have her number!

"Samir!" I hear her voice and immediately look up, trying to locate her through the sound.

And there she stands, a few steps away, waving at me with a wide grin on her face.

SHE NEARLY RIPPED MY HEART OUT AND NOW SHE IS SMILING! SERIOUSLY!

I walk toward her. "Where were you? Do you have any idea how worried I was?" I almost shout, but then I see the fear in her round eyes, and my anger softens. "I'm sorry," I mumble. "By the way, what are you doing here?"

"Check out this place! It's packed with all sorts of street food. You haven't been in Bangladesh for ages, so why not try out all of these?" she suggests.

I smile awkwardly. "Well, these foods can be quite spicy"

"So what? As a real Bengali, you gotta have the guts to handle some heat. Otherwise, you're missing out on the Bengali experience!" She stands tall in front of me.

She.is.adorable.

"Alright, let's do it," I agree.

Her smile widens. "First stop, Jhalmuri!" She points to a little stall selling Jhalmuri.

It's a famous street food here. It's a mix of puffed rice, spices, onions, tomatoes, and a bunch of other flavourful ingredients.

"I've tried jhalmuri recently. It wasn't spicy." I say as we stroll along together.

"But this one is different! It's got extra fiery chilies,"

"No way, Aleena! I'm not putting myself through that torture!"

"Oh, yes, you are!"

"I'm telling you, I'm not!"

"You are!"

SEVEN
ALEENA

The morning is just like any other for me. Waking up, feeling hungry and running out of the room, while Sara is still snoozing away. As I make my way to the kitchen, I notice some of Sara's aunts. "Umm hello?" I speak in an attempt to grab their attention.

Their eyes turn at me and soon gentle smiles occupy their lips, sending sudden warmth through my chest. "Aleena, right?" one of them asks with a smile whom I haven't met the day I arrived.

"Uh yes," I reply.

"Bhabi was talking about you today. She went out to do some wedding shopping, but she told us she wants you to have breakfast as soon as you wake up." I grin. "How thoughtful of her. Also, thank you."

"No worries dear. Where is Sara, by the way?"

"She hasn't woken up yet."

"Okay. Come here. I'll prepare food for you."

At her words, I slowly step further, ephemerally adjusting myself amidst them. "Auntie, let me help you," I offer. "Not a chance, Aleena! You are our guest, how can we get you to work? You can sit there and wait till your food prepares," she answers with a smile. However, I'm unable to bear the possibility of simply staying there doing nothing while they work tirelessly in the kitchen.

"Auntie, please let me lend a hand," I request again, hoping she will agree this time. She hesitates for a moment, considering my request but eventually she smiles. "Alright, Aleena. If you insist, you can help us. We could use an extra set of hands. But before that, have your food"

"Okay!"

I dip the paratha into the mouthwatering curry and then shove a large piece into my mouth, while I watch the Auntie cooking biryani. "This looks absolutely delicious!"

She smiles. "That's why I received this special request from Samir to cook it. He is a huge fan of my homemade Biryani."

As soon as I hear his name, a rosy blush paints my cheeks. I take another bite of the paratha, trying my best not to blush.

"You should try the paratha with tea," She suggests. "With tea? We never eat paratha like that." I smile nervously, causing her to chuckle. "In Chattogram, we mostly eat paratha dipped in tea. It might sound weird to you, but trust me, it's delicious."

I chuckle in response.

I focus in and join them in the kitchen after I finish my breakfast. She hands me a wooden spoon, and I help her in cooking the Biryani.

♡

I and Sara walk into the dining room, where we notice our parents and Sara's extended family already gathered around the grand dining table for dinner. And that's when Sahil Bhaiya joins us, and we all take our seats, with Sara sitting between me and Sahil Bhaiya.

"Sahil, where is Samir?" Sara's dad asks.

"I called him, he is coming." He replies immediately

"Here I am!" all of our eyes land at Samir, who just enters the dining room with a slight smile hanging on his face. Soon he greets the elders. "Come dear, sit," my mom offers. Smiling at her, he casts his eyes to spot an empty chair and eventually his gaze stops at the only empty chair next to me.

Stepping closer, he leans in. "May I?" he asks, in a hushed voice.

His concern for my comfort, even when it's his own home, leaves me surprised. The way he treats me, being gentle and respectful, makes me drawn to him even more.

As we start to eat, all of our attention comes to Samir shortly after we hear his voice. "Chachi, your Biryani is the best as always!"

Everyone, including his Aunt, smiles at his words. "Thank you dear, but this time someone else helped me."

Her words make me stop chewing my food as I realize she's talking about me.

Samir's eyebrows raise up to his aunt as confusion takes over his face. "Who are you talking about, Chachi?"

"The person sitting next to you."

Once Samir hears his Aunt, his eyes swiftly move to me.

"That's why the Biryani tastes even more delicious today," Samir whispers, drawing my attention towards him. But he seems engrossed in his meal, as if he hadn't said anything surprising. I can't be certain if I misheard it or if he actually said it, but when I catch a glimpse of a smile playing on his lips, my heart races, dispelling all my confusions.

What did he mean by that?!

Is he being nice to me once again, just because I'm his sister's best friend?

The thought rings in my mind as I fiddle with the spoon on my plate.

"Bhaiya, you're freaking her out again! But wait, he didn't do anything to scare you," Sara says, noticing my shocked face. Samir, on the other hand, puts on this puzzled look, acting like he's just as confused as she is. But deep down, I know he's totally messing with me this time.

"Yeah right. But did I really scare you again?" he asks with an innocent look, all while making sure Sara remains oblivious.

But I ignore him and do my best to hold back the nervousness crawling up my body, and instead, I focus on my food.

I quickly cast a glance at my best friend, who's seated on the other end of the sofa, engrossed in showcasing the clothes we bought just a few days ago. "Mom, check this one out. Aleena helped me choose it," Sara exclaims, picking up a shopping bag and handing it to her mother.

Her mom's face beams with a smile as she carefully examines the delicate fabric. "Oh, my dear, this one is absolutely beautiful! You truly have such impeccable taste, Aleena," she praises, her eyes lifting to meet my gaze. A shy smile tugs at the corners of my lips.

"No doubt, Mom. My bestie has the best taste! Just wait and see, she'll choose the perfect guy for herself as her husband,"

I chuckle at Sara's words.

"Don't get too excited, my dear bestie! Even if you choose someone, I'll still have to put him through a series of tests.

Can't let just anyone marry my precious best friend, you know? He has to pass my tests before I give him permission to marry you."

I prop my elbow on the sofa's arm and lean forward a little. "Alright, My mom, I won't get married until you give me the permission."

"Look, Samir, what they are talking about. And your sister has gone completely mad!" Sara's mom interrupts, chuckling.

My eyes widen and my fingers instinctively clench into fists as I swallow hard, slowly turning my head to see who's standing behind me. And there he is, Samir, standing tall with his hands in his pockets. His head tilts downward to meet my gaze, and there it is, a pair of dimples forming on his cheeks. I feel my breath catch in my throat.

"Son, come on, take a seat. See what your sister got while shopping," his mom calls out.

"Mom, I actually have some work to do," he replies.

"Please, Bhaiya! Just sit for ten minutes! I want to show you something," Sara pleads, and Samir knows he can't go back on his sister's word anymore.

He walks past me and settles down next to Sara, sitting directly across from me. "You carry on. I'll go and check on the other preparations," their mom says, getting up and leaving the room.

"Bhaiya, look at this one."

Samir looks at the clothes his sister is showing him, exchanging words with her and awkwardly avoiding eye contact with me every time our eyes unintentionally meet.

To dodge making eye contact with him, I whip out my phone and scroll through it. Just then, a message pops up on the screen. Opening the chat, a smile forms on my face as I read the meme my cousin has sent me.

"Aleena, who's got you grinning from ear to ear on your phone, huh?" Sara leans in, showing off the most playful and teasing smile she can muster.

Samir pauses. His eyes shoot up to me. But by then, I've already managed to redirect my attention towards his sister. "What's with that smile Sara!"

My eyes dart to Samir, who has already locked his eyes on me. He doesn't utter a single word, just stares. And this sudden attention sends a tingling sensation rippling throughout my body.

"What's going on?" Sara asks again, this time with an even more mischievous tone.

But I can only feel myself melting from within as I sense Samir's eyes burning into me. Swiftly, I flip my phone, showing the screen to Sara, knowing well that Samir can also clearly view it. "It's my cousin. She sent me this meme."

But then a burst of uncontrollable laughter erupts from Sara. "Girl, what did you think I would actually doubt about you? I knew you'd be smiling at any meme. I was just messing with you."

I stare at my best friend blankly. The fading sound of Sara's laughter is replaced by an awkward silence that hangs in the air.

"Sorry," She says softly.

"I'm running late, I should get going." Samir speaks up, catching our attention. He gives me one last look and walks away with a straight face, leaving me sitting there, utterly dumbfounded.

What's wrong with him suddenly?

EIGHT
SAMIR

I step out of the house and head straight to the car, settling myself in the driver's seat and gripping the steering wheel tight. Without a clue where I'm going, I speed off, feeling all kinds of messed up inside.

What's wrong with me?

Why am I feeling like this?

Why did I feel like my heart was getting ripped out when at that moment I thought she's got someone in her life?

Why am I so concerned about what's going on in her life?

It's her life, her choice.

I shouldn't be dwelling on it. I shouldn't be dwelling on her.

This restlessness in my heart, it's driving me crazy.

I've never felt like this before.

What has been going on since the day I met her?

Countless questions swirl within my mind, but I'm unable to find the answers. Perhaps deep down, I already know the truth, but fear holds me back from admitting it. Everything is just not making sense. We just met, and things shouldn't be going down this path. It's not what I initially think it is, or maybe I have to convince myself otherwise.

♡

I walk over to the open balcony, right next to the living room, and plop down on a chair. Aleena, Sara and some of our other cousins are there, busy wrapping the gifts in the dalas we bought earlier. I can tell Aleena noticed me coming out here, but I purposely avoid making eye contact, trying to avoid those weird feelings from creeping back in. I sit there in silence for a good ten minutes, until I sense someone slowly approaching me.

In the next moment, Aleena settles down in the chair right next to mine, leaving a little gap between us. She attaches her knees together and rests her hands on top of them. "Hey."

I manage to force a smile. "Hi"

And then, the silence wraps around us. We sit there, not saying a word, as if the quiet has swallowed us whole.

Finally she breaks the awkwardness between us. "What happened?" she asks.

I steal a quick glance at her, then shift my gaze to the sky outside the balcony, and then back to her again. "What's gonna happen to me? I'm totally fine," I say, trying to act all cool. But she doesn't seem to buy it, and her expression says it all.

"Why did you walk out suddenly like that yesterday? And then you ignored me the rest of the day. And even now. What's wrong?" she asks, her voice filled with concern.

"I told you it's nothing."

"Did I do anything wrong?"

"Aleena, it's nothing. I was just caught up with things yesterday, and I may have unintentionally given the impression that I was ignoring you."

"Being busy, and intentionally avoiding are not the same thing. I can sense that something's bothering you. I know you. You were never like this before." she says, her eyes searching mine.

This time I look directly into her eyes. "Please.... Please, stop knowing me so well. Stop understanding me, stop wondering what's going on inside me. Don't make it hard for me. I don't want to deviate from what I'm forcing myself to believe."

She gazes at me, all confused and unable to understand what I'm saying. But my voice, my intense gaze, and the emotions etched on my face convey everything she needs to know—it's about her. She falls silent, her eyes fixated on me.

"Aleena, what are you doing here? We still gotta wrap more gifts! Let's go!" Sara barges in but then her voice trails off as her eyes travel between me and Aleena.

"Aleena" She calls out again but this time in a lower voice.

Without even sparing a glance in my direction, I watch Aleena walk out with Sara.

I guess I deserved it, didn't I?

Later that evening, I make my way to Sara's room and give a gentle knock on the door. Within seconds, Sara opens the door. "Bhaiya?" she voices, questioning my presence.

"Where is Aleena?" I ask.

She takes a moment to respond, and her gaze drifts over to her bed. I follow her eyes and there she is—Aleena, sitting right there. As our eyes meet, I can see a frown forming on her face. "Um, can I talk to you?" I ask, hoping she'll be up for it.

I'm aware that my sister is also in the room, and I can sense the awkwardness in Aleena's eyes for the same reason. But right now, I don't want to dwell on that. All I want is to have a conversation with her, which is why I'm here in my sister's room. "It won't take long,"

Aleena glances at Sara, then back at me.

"Aleena, go on and check out what bhaiya wants to talk about." Sara says. This time, Aleena slowly nods. "I'm coming."

A wide smile lights up my face. "I'm waiting for you out on the balcony,"

I head down to the kitchen, make up two cups of coffee. Balancing the warm cups in my hands, I return to the balcony. Soon enough, I sense footsteps drawing closer, and I turn around to see Aleena standing right beside me, leaning against the glass railing with a bit of distance between us.

Extending my hand, I offer her the other cup of coffee. "You made it?" she asks.

"Yes, just after I went to call you," I reply.

I catch a glimpse of her taking the first sip from the cup. "It's too bitter!" she exclaims and her face scrunches up a little.

"I thought you might like it" I say, taking the cup from her and placing it gently on the nearby coffee table.

"And what made you think like that?"

"Sara always goes for this Americano, usually iced. So I assumed you might have a similar taste," I explain, taking a sip from my own cup.

She smiles. "Your logic doesn't quite make sense."

"Why not? I've heard that best friends often share similar preferences."

This time, she turns around, pressing her back against the railing. "Well, maybe not in our case."

I just chuckle in response.

The air grows heavy with a sudden silence that wraps around us. We stand there, not uttering a single word. And then, I finally gather up the courage to say those words that have been swirling around in my head. "I'm really sorry about earlier. My mind was all messed up because of something,"

"And what's that something?" She asks, but I can't bring myself to spill the reason in front of her, so I just stay quiet. Soon enough, I hear her laughing. "You don't need to say it. I was just messing with you"

I trace the edge of my cup with my thumb.

"So, it seems you have a distaste for bitter flavors,"

"Yeah, I can't stand anything bitter, whether it's the coffee or the words people say." Her response sends a pang of guilt through me once again. "I'm really sorry."

In the next moment, she bursts out laughing again. "I was just kidding," she says, pausing for a moment before continuing, "I'm not mad at you, and I wasn't mad at that moment either. I could tell something was bothering you, and I understood that your reaction was a result of that, not because you wanted to react that way."

I glance at her, locking eyes in silence, not saying a word. Her eyebrows furrow. "What?" she asks.

I quickly avert my gaze. "It's nothing. I was just thinking whether I should stop letting my mind take the lead and start listening to my heart instead."

She listens to me carefully and then gives me a smile. "Well, you know what? You should ask yourself which decision makes you happier. Is it the one your mind tells you or the one your heart tells you?"

I gaze at her as she concludes her words, her undivided attention fixed on me. "It's my heart," I confess, keeping my gaze steady on her. "I find happiness in what my heart whispers to me."

She smiles. "Then listen to your heart"

We stay there a bit longer, chatting about whatever comes to mind. And then, she walks away, leaving me behind with the empty cup of coffee in my hand.

NINE

ALEENA

I take a sip of tea from my cup and look up at the cloudy sky. My fingers around the cup tighten as a cool breeze gently caresses my face. When I went back to Sara last night, I thought she'd ask me a bunch of questions about Samir. But surprisingly she didn't even ask a single question and acted like Samir was never there, like he never even called me to talk in front of her.

"I was looking for you the whole house, and you are here sitting alone," Sara says, sitting next to me.

"Yes, I wanted to enjoy this amazing morning. And you were sleeping, so I didn't want to disturb you," I reply, catching a glimpse of my best friend.

She wraps her arms around me and rests her head on my shoulder. "I was thinking about something. After the wedding ends, you're going to go back to your home, and we will go back to the US. Then what will I do?"

"What is that supposed to mean? We will return to our normal schedules," I answer, giggling.

"But I'll miss you so much." A cute pout forms on her lips as she voices her words. "Aww, my bestie, I'll miss you too." I gently squeeze her cheek.

"I don't want you to go," Sara adds, making me giggle once again. "So tell me, Sara Zafar, what am I going to do then?" The question makes her pause for a moment. She places her chin on her hand and ponders about something until her eyes widen and she looks back at me. "I've got an idea."

"Yes, please, go ahead."

"A simple one. Marry Samir Bhaiya and be my Bhabi. Then you can stay with us forever, and I can meet you every day."

I freeze in my place, unsure of how to react or respond. But there is my best friend, who is staring at me with such hope as if she had just asked me for the simplest thing. "Dumb girl! Do you know what you are saying!?"

Noticing my shocked reaction, Sara chuckles. "Achha, achha, calm down. I was just joking. But the idea was good tho-" She can't finish her words as she receives a glare from me.

Adjusting my clothes, I get up from the bench, clutching my phone in one hand and a cup in the other. "Where are you going?" Sara asks. "My phone's dead. I need to charge it," I swiftly respond and dart into the house, not wanting my best friend to witness my red face caused by her shocking idea.

I'm on my way to Sara's room, but abruptly I notice Sara's mom struggling with a bunch of shopping bags in her hand. "Auntie, why are you carrying so many bags? You could've asked someone's help."

"Don't worry, dear; I can manage it. Others are busy with other preparations, so I don't want to tire anyone out," she replies, gentleness in her voice. "Aunty, give all these to me. I'll carry," I offer, hoping she would agree to let me help.

"No Aleena. I can manage."

"How can I leave you like this? Just tell me where to keep all these," I ask, taking all the bags from her.

"Thank you so much, sweetheart. Just go straight and then left. There is another guest room. Keep all these bags there."

With all the bags in my hands, I walk toward the direction Sara's mom has pointed me to. I haven't explored this part of the house yet, so everything is unfamiliar to me.

As I reach the assigned area, I notice two rooms. I'm not sure which one is the guest room since one entryway is open and the other is shut. I choose not to open the closed door and enter the room that is opened.

I place some bags on the couch and the rest on the bed. "Carrying these bags is really tiring," I murmur to myself and look at the empty side of the bed. Carelessly, I let my body sink onto the bed for a couple of minutes. And it's OKAY for me to rest on the bed since it's a guest room and no one is using it at the moment. I close my eyes and stretch my arms wide.

"Is the bed comfortable?" A familiar voice startles me and prompts me to glance at its source. My eyes are about to pop out of their sockets when I notice Samir leaning against the doorway of what appears to be a dressing room.

"What are you doing here?" I ask as I slide down the bed, stand straight, and fix my clothes. His hands are tucked inside his jeans pocket, and I can see a smirk emerging on his lips.

"Isn't that what I was supposed to ask you? What are you doing in my room?"

There you go, congratulations to me for walking into the wrong room!

"This is your room?"

His eyebrows arch as he tilts his head slightly. "Yes, it is."

"I'm sorry, I... I thought this was the guest room your mom mentioned." I try to clarify, hoping he will believe my words, but I notice him walking toward me while he lets the smirk still linger on his lips.

"The room next to mine, that's the guest room," he says as he continues stepping closer to me. Rather than escaping, I remain and do whatever it takes not to be impacted by his abrupt action. And he doesn't seem to care either, even as I watch him approach me.

He finally stops, standing a couple of inches away, with his hands directly sliding into his pockets. My hands squeeze into fists, trying desperately to stop the rapid thumping of my heart, but I don't utter a word.

His head sways slightly, attempting to catch my gaze, which ultimately turns out to be a futile effort. "Am I scaring you again?" His hushed words, accompanied by his warm breath that brushes against my face, send sudden shivers down my body.

At this very moment, I'm not quite able to comprehend the fluttery sensation I'm feeling inside me. But I can acutely feel the heat rising to my cheeks as the sound of my own heartbeat grows louder.

The bracelet on my wrist can't handle the fast and irregular rhythm of my racing heart, as it has a special feature that can detect my heartbeat. And soon the alarm on the bracelet goes off loudly, catching both of our attention.

Our eyes drop to the bracelet.

As my eyes return to him, I see his gaze still fixed on my hand. There's a glint of shock in his eyes, and I realize that he has acknowledged the effect he's having on me.

His surprised eyes meet mine, and he intuitively takes a step back. His face is scratched with a blend of confusion and curiosity, as if he has just discovered something he had never thought of. Sensing the opportunity, I swiftly run out of his room.

TEN

ALEENA

I gaze at the bracelet wrapped around my wrist. "Why did I even wear it?! Ugh! For this stupid bracelet, I had to face that embarrassment!" I flop onto the bed, letting my frustration out by tossing and turning restlessly. I'm about to remove it when suddenly my hands halt as a thought rings into my mind. "But this bracelet has forever been in my hand. I don't want to remove it. Crap! What will I do!?"

The door opens and Sara barges in, roaming her eyes around. As her eyes drop on me, a wide smile captures her lips. "Aleena, my cousins, means my Khala's sons are here, let's go. I'll introduce you to them."

"Calm down, bestie. You look super excited," I say, chuckling. "After all, I'm gonna introduce my one and only best friend to them!"

"Okay, let's go."

We make our way down the stairs to the lawn. I notice two men around my age sitting nearby, along with Samir and Sahil bhaiya. Seeing Samir there, the memory of the morning flashes before my eyes, yet I somehow manage to stay calm. "Aleena, meet my cousins Yasir and Asif. And brothers, this is Aleena, my best friend," Sara introduces them.

"Aleena... Hmmm... Your name is as pretty as you," Yasir says, flashing a flirty smile, but surprisingly, it doesn't make me nervous or shy. I remain unfazed and brush it off with a laugh.

Soon I join the group and start chatting with them, intentionally ignoring Samir. Being the extrovert that I am, I fully immerse myself in the conversation with Sara's cousins, and honestly I feel so happy at this moment.

However, I notice Samir's eyes on me multiple times, and he seems somewhat upset.

What's wrong with him?

Just when I'm about to turn away from him, he speaks up, drawing everyone's attention. "Umm, Aleena, you left your ring in my room earlier," he hauls my ring out of his pocket.

I sit there frozen.

My eyes widen.

The whole atmosphere falls into a shocked silence as everyone's eyes are fixed on me and Samir. After all, the combination of me, him, my ring, and his room is truly unexpected for everyone.

I look down at my finger, only to realize that the ring isn't really there. An awkward chuckle escapes my lips. "Umm... Actually, I went to his room to drop off some shopping bags, and I accidentally left it there" I explain as my eyes travel to each of them. "But why in bhaiya's room?" Sara asks.

"Indeed, Aleena, tell them, why in my room?" Samir adds, a smile playing on his lips. All I can do is glare at him, but he seems to be having a good time.

"Actually, I accidentally went to his room thinking it was the guest room," I answer.

"So many accidents!" he says with a dramatic sigh.

He's totally doing it on purpose!

"Surprise!"

All of us fall silent and look back.

"Apu! When did you come?" Sara exclaims, running to a lady standing nearby. "Just now," she replies briefly with a smile. In her arms, she cradles a one-year-old baby, while a man stands next to her.

"Aleena, meet my cousin Mubashira Apu, her husband Eshan bhaiya, and their adorable baby Saad," Sara introduces them.

Mubashira smiles. "Hi, Aleena."

I return her smile, briefly glancing at her adorable son cradled in her arms before focusing back on her.

"I've heard so much about you from Sara" she adds.

"Okay, did she bring me up to every single person she knows?" I cast a dramatic glance at Sara, prompting chuckles from both Mubashira Apu and Sara. "Well, that could be possible," Sara replies, mirroring my theatrical tone.

We stand there exchanging a few more words until Mubashira Apu asks, "Guys, is Mom inside?"

"Yes, go ahead; Chachi is inside," Samir replies right away.

"Alright, I'll go and meet everyone. I'll be back to join you soon."

After Mubashira Apu and her family come back, we all settle in. "Finally, it's wedding season! I can't express how happy I am for you, Sahil," Mubashira Apu exclaims and Sahil bhaiya smiles in response.

Just as she begins to engage in conversation with everyone, her son suddenly starts crying in her arms. "Well, duty calls. You all carry on, I need to calm him down." With that, she walks back into the house.

"Aleena, let's go, I've something to show you" Sara says all of a sudden, grabbing my wrist.

As we walk inside the house, I feel something is missing in my hand and in the next moment I realize that I have left her phone outside. "Sara, I left my phone there, you go ahead, I'll be joining you"

"Okay. Come fast!"

I quickly go back, pick up my phone, and see four of the men still there.

As I'm about to head back, I suddenly hear Samir's voice. I turn around and see him striding towards me, until he stands right in front of me. "You forgot to take your ring," he says.

I catch a glimpse of the ring on his hand and swiftly retrieve it. "I gotta g-" before I can even finish my words, Yasir appears out of nowhere. "Hey, Aleena."

I glance at Samir and then back at Yasir. "Umm, hi."

"If you're cool with it, can I get your number? You know, it's a wedding house. Just in case you need any help, I'll be there in a flash if you give me a call." My eyes nearly widen at his words as I clearly perceive his motive behind asking for my number.

Yet again, I glance back at Samir and he looks seriously pissed off. At this point, I really want him to speak up because, obviously, I'm not going to share my number. Moreover, I can't come up with any solutions on how to tackle the situation.

Samir throws his arm around Yasir's neck, but his smile seems a bit forced. "Yasir, you haven't eaten properly since you came. Let's go and eat again."

"But wait-" Yasir tries to stay back, but Samir cuts him off. "You are not listening to your older brother? Remember I'm one and half years older than you. Now listen to your bhaiya! Let's go!"

Not giving Yasir a chance to say anything, Samir swiftly whisks him away. I stand there, laughing at the sight before me. But then he suddenly catches me staring, and I quickly avert my eyes, feeling super embarrassed.

ELEVEN
ALEENA

"Sara, move over a bit!" I nudge my best friend, hoping to claim my share of mirror space.

"You move!"

"Almost done! Just give me a sec," I say, quickly fixing my kameez, bangles, and adjusting my jhumkas.

I step back, allowing Sara to take over the mirror completely. "Okay, you can have the whole mirror now!"

"But don't you dare leave without me! I had to start late just for you, you know!" Sara says, causing me to chuckle. "Take your time. I'm here!"

I walk up to the window and take a peek at the amazing decorations of the Mehedi ceremony. The lawn below is all lit up with sparkling lights, creating a mesmerizing sight. A smile lights up my face as I see people arriving in their most splendid attire.

Once Sara is ready, we head downstairs and catch a glimpse of the groom, who's already all set to make his entrance. Everyone is gathered there. Right next to Sahil bhaiya, I notice Samir standing there, looking absolutely perfect in his Green Panjabi.

Our eyes meet. I can feel the warmth in his gaze, as if our eyes are having their own secret conversation, silently praising each other.

Sara makes some adjustments to Sahil bhaiya's outfit, while Samir fixes his hair. After all, they want their brother to look his absolute best for this special day. The camera crew stands prepared, ready to capture every precious moment. Sahil bhaiya makes his grand entrance, and we're right there by his side, soaking up the excitement and cheering along with everyone else.

Once Sahil bhaiya takes his place on the stage, I grab Sara's wrist and drag her to the food stall on the side. "Fuchka!" I exclaim happily, spotting plates of fuchka lined up on the long table. It's a crispy round shell, stuffed with a tangy and spicy mixture.

And right next to it, there's a person making Jilapi. It is a famous Bengali crispy sweet treat, coated in sugar syrup.

"Uncle, please add extra spices," I request.

Sara shoots me a disappointed look, shaking her head. "Seriously, Aleena, how do you eat so much spicy food? I can't even tolerate that."

I laugh. "You have no clue how to handle spicy food!"

"I know! Enjoy your extra spicy fuchka and I happily indulge in my favorite Jilapi!"

Our food preferences are different: I love spicy foods, and Sara loves sweet foods (And sometimes bitter!). But that doesn't change the fact that we are still best friends.

We keep chuckling and prodding each other while stuffing the food into our mouths.

TWELVE

SAMIR

My phone buzzes in my hand. I quickly flip it over to check the caller ID and in the next moment I answer it. "Hello, Mr. Smith, I was just about to call you." I say but his voice doesn't seem to reach me clearly. "Hello?" I repeat.

"I guess it's just a network problem, give me a couple of minutes." I make my way to the lawn, hoping for a better signal. "Yes, now I can hear you. So, as I was saying, I'm planning a small meeting to discuss the interior and everything..." I pause for a moment, as I catch a glimpse of Aleena sitting there with my sister. I quickly refocus on our call and continue discussing the remaining details before wrapping it up.

I look back at Aleena and propel myself towards her. Even though I should probably be heading back to my room and getting some work done. But it was her who told me to trust my heart's instincts. So, I guess I'm just going with the flow. And work can wait right?

As I approach them, their conversation gradually becomes clearer to my ears.

"I gotta tell ya, the Mehedi night was freaking awesome! Like, how much fun we had last night!" Sara exclaims.

"Indeed. I miss it already" Mubashira Apu adds.

"I hope I'm not interrupting something" I plop myself down on a chair nearby.

Mubashira apu chuckles. "No you're absolutely not"

"We were just talking about last night. Wasn't it an incredible time?" she asks.

I nod, unable to resist stealing glances at Aleena. And she's gazing right back at me, her eyes fixed, as if she's lost in a world of her own.

"Aleena, you seem so lost," I say.

My words, spoken innocently in front of Sara and Mubashira, carry a hidden meaning that only Aleena can decipher. And I know exactly how I make her feel.

"Umm… No… I'm totally okay," she replies, forcing a smile.

However, the moment soon comes to an end as Mubashira apu speaks, bringing up another topic. "Listen, remember when we came here last time and witnessed that breathtaking sunrise? Let's go and watch it again!"

"Count me in," I reply and Sara also nods in agreement.

I turn my gaze towards Aleena, waiting for her response, hoping that she'll have the same answer as the rest of us.

"Umm, you all go ahead. I'm not sure if I'll join or not." she hesitates.

"Why, Aleena? Hear me out, Chattogram is a city of hills, you know there are a lot of stunning sunrise spots. You really should see them," Sara insists.

"Come on, it'll be so much fun!" Mubashira apu adds.

Aleena looks back at me once again, and I can tell she understands what I'm silently asking of her.

Please say you're coming with us.

Please say you're coming with us.

"Okay, I'll join," she finally says. And then her eyes shift from me to Sara.

I smile, wide enough for her to notice it.

As the conversation comes to a close, we make our way back into the house. I walk up the stairs, with Aleena right in front of me and Sara right next to her. Suddenly, a strong grip seizes our wrists, swiftly pulling us into a room. As our eyes scan the surroundings, we realize we're in Sara's room. And there she stands, arms folded, gazing intently at me and Aleena with her piercing eyes.

I arch my eyebrows. "What's the matter, Sara?"

But she just stares at us, her eyes going back and forth between me and Aleena, like she's trying to figure out some crazy riddle. "I should be asking you both: What's happening between you two?" she asks.

I shift my gaze to the side, stealing a quick glance at Aleena. With my arms folded, I try my best to suppress the smile that threatens to break free. But Aleena just stands there, frozen and wide-eyed. But then she manages to let out an awkward laugh. "Sara, what are you talking about?"

Sara shoots her a sarcastic smile. "Come on now, don't try to pull the wool over my eyes. I'm a psychology student. I can read your expressions like an open book. That expression on your face and the tremble in your voice give it all away. But still, I want to hear it from both of you."

I awkwardly smile, as if the woman standing before me is no longer my younger sister, but my mother. "Sara, what made you think like that?"

Sara's eyebrows shoot up with a proud expression as she turns her gaze back to me. "I've been observing everything. Since day one. My bestie really gets lost into you a lot. I mean, it's so obvious."

"I-I- just remembered something. I gotta go." The words tumble out of Aleena's mouth, and before Sara can stop her, she hastily makes her way out of the room, leaving the us alone there.

I sit on the edge of the bed, ready to answer Sara's questions. I know evading her inquiries is futile. Besides, I want to be honest with her about my feelings for Aleena.

Sara scrutinizes my expression until she finally decides to ask. "Do you like her?"

My eyes briefly meet my sister's, a mix of emotions rushing inside me, before I avert my gaze, unable to find the answer within myself. "It's complicated," I answer, my voice barely above a whisper.

Her arms loosen from their folds, falling straight to her sides. "What do you mean, Bhaiya? Look, I don't know what's going on inside you, but Aleena... she is my best friend, and I don't want to see her heartbroken because of you."

I sit there in silence.

"What's really going on with you, Bhaiya?" Sara asks.

I tilt my head down ever so slightly. "I don't know what it is, but when I catch a glimpse of her, all I want to do is keep staring at her. When I hear her voice, it's like my heart is embraced by a gentle warmth. When I see her with another man, it's like a thousand tiny blades piercing my heart, tearing me apart from the inside. Just the mere thought of her leaving fills me with a sudden fear. Even when she is not around me, she still lingers in my mind, a constant presence that I can't escape."

There is a brief moment of silence, and then I look up at my sister.

Her eyes widens. "No way!" she mutters and then smiles slightly. "It's...It's called LOVE, my brother."

She takes a gentle step forward, closing the distance between us, and settles herself beside me. "I have seen it in your eyes when you spoke of her. I've heard it in your voice, the way it trembled with emotion,"

"But.. We just met. It hasn't been that long."

"Love doesn't play by the rules of time. If she is truly the one for you, time just becomes irrelevant. Sometimes all it takes is a single encounter that can turn your whole world upside down," she pauses before continuing again. "I might not have any experience with falling in love. But this is something I strongly believe."

I steal a quick glance at my sister, and a soft chuckle escapes my lips. "It's kinda weird, you giving me advice,"

"Come on, bhaiya, there's nothing wrong with it," she says and I chuckle along with her.

"At the end of the day, it's your life and Aleena's. Whatever decision you make, I hope you stick to it and never have any regrets." she adds.

I remain silent and then nod slowly.

THIRTEEN
ALEENA

"Sara, hurry up!" I shout, standing by Samir's car with Mubashira Apu. The sun hadn't risen yet, haziness is surrounding us as we wait for Sara to show up. We doze for a couple of hours before getting ready to go to watch the sunrise.

"By the way Apu, won't you take your baby and Eshan Bhaiya?" I ask, draping my arms around myself.

"Saad will annoy me a lot if I wake him up now. And Eshan was like 'Nah I need my beauty sleep'. So I left Saad with him," she replies.

In the next moment, we notice Samir stepping out, wearing white denim with a black t-shirt underneath and paired with a black jeans. With each step down the small stairs, his silky, wavy hair sways, adding a touch of irresistible charm.

What a sight!

His gaze meets mine, and a warm smile instantly lights up his face, as if he's genuinely happy to see me. Then he exchanges smiles with Mubashira Apu, patiently waiting for Sara to join us.

And finally, Sara shows up.

Since it is winter, the morning air has a slight chill, but strangely enough, I don't feel the need to bundle up in warm clothing.

"Aleena, I'm telling you again! You'll freeze out there. Please, just take something," Sara urges.

"Don't worry, I won't feel cold," I reply, managing to shut my best friend up.

"Girls, wait a minute! I forgot something. I'll go and get it." Samir says all of a sudden and dashes into the house.

In less than five minutes, he comes back, clutching another jacket.

"Bhaiya, why did you take another one?" Sara knits her eyebrows.

He glances at me and then turns his attention back to Sara. "I was actually torn between this jacket and the one I'm wearing. Once we get there, I'll check if this one matches the view. If it doesn't, I'll switch to the other one."

Sara and Mubashira apu sigh. "You and your fashion sense, always so particular!"

As we approach the car, I decide to take a seat in the back with Mubashira apu. But just as I am about to do so, Sara interrupts, using her cute voice to plead with me, "Aleena, babe, can you please sit in the front? I'm still so sleepy and just wanna lay back and snooze until we reach our destination. You can join me in the back, but I don't want Samir bhaiya to scold me, saying, 'I'm not your driver!'"

Her playful imitation of Samir cracks me up.

Without any further hesitation, she swiftly slides into the car, resting her head on Mubashira Apu's lap. Since Mubashira Apu is already settled in the back, I don't want to bother to ask her to switch seats.

I glance at Samir, who patiently waits for me in the car, his eyebrows slightly raised, silently questioning why I haven't hopped in yet. I take a deep breath, trying to calm myself, and finally settle myself into the front seat.

FOURTEEN
SAMIR

I fix my hair and check myself out in the mirror one more time. I opt for a black t-shirt paired with black pants. To top it off, I slide into a white denim jacket. The day is special for me because Aleena is joining us. I quickly stash my phone in my pocket and grab my shades before heading out.

Just as my eyes land on Aleena, I stop.

She looks absolutely adorable.

What catches my attention the most is the small clip she has delicately placed in the side of her wavy hair.

Samir, Calm down.

Calm down.

Calm your heart.

After a few minutes, Sara finally shows up, and we're about to get in the car when I hear her abrupt voice. "Aleena, I'm telling you again! You'll freeze out there. Please, just take something," Sara insists. But Aleena brushes off her concern. "Don't worry, I won't feel cold."

My eyes flicker between Aleena and Sara, taking in every detail of what's happening. I stand there, contemplating something. And then, at a point, I take a little step back, gearing up to actually go ahead with whatever I have in mind.

"Girls, wait a minute! I forgot something. I'll go and get it." I say before running back into the house and heading straight to my room.

My fingers brush over the jackets hanging in my cupboard until they land on the one. Yeah, my favorite blue jacket. I know it'll be enough to shield Aleena from the cold.

As I step out, jacket in hand, I know I'm gonna face a bunch of questions. I can already imagine the puzzled looks and curious inquiries from the three of them, but I somehow manage to come up with a fashion-related excuse to end the conversation.

Once we settle into my car, I overhear Sara asking Aleena to take the front seat while she happily takes her place in the back. I break into a smile as I glance back at my sister, who's giving me a cheeky look with her wiggling eyebrows.

Finally, our journey begins with Aleena sitting right next to me. The ride is quiet and I notice Sara already dozed off with her head on Mubashira Apu's lap.

I steal a quick glance at Aleena, only to find her gazing outside, enjoying the beauty of nature with a gentle smile gracing her lips. Our eyes meet for a fleeting moment, and then she looks away. I can feel a sudden nervousness within us but I choose to remain silent.

As we arrive at our destination, we all step out of the car. I glance at my watch to check the time and realize the sunrise is just a mere fifteen minutes away. I look over at Aleena and notice her body trembling and she swiftly hugs herself tight, trying to fight off the chill.

"See! That is the reason I told you to take something warm! But you didn't listen to me! Anyways, come here and stick with me, maybe it will help you," Sara offers, thinking about sharing her sweater with Aleena, but it's clear that it wouldn't be enough to warm her up.

Aleena shakes her head, "No, Sara. It won't help. Instead, it will make you feel cold. It's okay."

This time I quickly dash back to the car, grab the jacket, and zoom back to her. "Here, take it. This will keep you warm."

Her eyes meet mine, and then she glances at the jacket in my hand. "But yo-"

"I don't need it, I won't change," I reply, hoping she will agree because I can't stand seeing her shivering like that for another second.

She smiles as she takes the jacket from me. "Thanks."

I watch her slide into the jacket and it's impossible for me to deny how incredibly cute and tiny she looks in it.

It melts my heart.

"Bhaiya, this is the first time ever! You never share your clothes, but today-" Sara goes speechless, her eyes widens as she tries to process what's happening.

Scratching the back of my neck, I flash an awkward smile and somehow manage to change the topic. "Hey, look! The sun will rise at any moment now!"

And that's when all of our gazes turn towards the sky. The sky is already displaying a beautiful array of colors, creating a breathtaking sight.

"THIS IS SO PRETTY!" Aleena exclaims.

I turn to look at her, and she's jumping up and down like a little kid. It's such a different side of her that I've never seen before, and it leaves me completely speechless.

She.is.so.adorable.

"Finally, you're back to being human!" Sara says, tapping Aleena's shoulder.

Mubashira apu chuckles. "What do you mean, Sara?"

"That cute, bubbly, cheerful Aleena is back, Apu! But whenever she is around Samir bhaiya, this side of her seems to vanish into thin air," Sara replies as if she just answered the most normal question, unaware that she put me and Aleena into a sudden awkward situation.

"I don't think so. I mean, we went shopping together and the night before that, we had a good chat," I say, trying to diffuse the awkwardness between us.

But I guess I messed up somehow.

Because the way Alena is giving me that look, it's definitely not the look someone would give if they're feeling happy.

"Wait, was I not supposed to say that?" I whisper to Aleena, even though I know Sara and Mubashira apu probably heard me too.

"No, no, haha, why not! I was hungry that night and Sara wasn't joining me, so I went to the kitchen alone and bumped into you by accident. Right Sara?" she asks, awkwardly laughing but my sister gives her an unbothered look. "How am I supposed to know if you bumped into him in the kitchen? You didn't tell me."

"Why do you always feel the need to explain?" I snap, feeling a bit annoyed. And honestly, I can't figure out why.

"Yes yes why? You even explained about that ring on bhaiya's bed" Sara adds looking completely innocent in front of her best friend.

"Bed!?" Mubashira Apu's eyes almost pop out.

"What's with that look! And how can you doubt my bestie's innocence" Sara says, giving her a serious look.

Well she sounds unserious too.

As I catch a glimpse of Aleena, I notice her cheeks turning a rosy shade once again.

"Why did you have to say that so loudly? You made things awkward," I say, glancing back at my sister.

"And why did you have to say it too? Just look at her. You've made her even more uncomfortable," she snaps back.

But as the sun starts to rise, our conversation slowly fades away. We fall into a peaceful silence as our eyes fixate on the sky.

"MashaAllah," Aleena whispers. Her eyes shimmers with tears of joy as she gazes at the sky.

I watch her silently.

The soft orange glow of the sun gently caresses her face making her even prettier that I can't take my eyes off her.

"MashaAllah," I whisper.

I watch her, as long as I can, as much as I can, but I can't get enough of it. And I know I can watch her like this for the rest of my life.

I feel different, definitely something more than special.

Now I know what my mind wants.

What my heart wants.

What every single inch of me wants.

It's her.

As we all stroll back to the car, ready to head home, I notice Mubashira Apu whispering something to Sara. In the next moment, Sara quietly settles in the backseat next to Mubashira apu. "Alee, sit up front again, please. I need to catch up on my sleep."

She rests her head on Mubashira apu's lap, leaving Aleena standing there, gazing at her best friend. And then she silently takes her place next to me. "Why do you sleep so much you sleepyhead!?" she exclaims, turning her head back.

"I have to make the most of my vacation by catching up on sleep! Once university reopens, I'll bid farewell to sleep. You'll never understand the struggles of a psychology student," Sara replies dramatically, with a sigh.

I chuckle. "Oh my sweetheart, then don't study and you can stay with us forever."

"No bhaiya! I know you all have given me a ton of love since childhood but I don't wanna be a BEKAR!" Sara's voice trails off into her sleep.

"You're cute!" Aleena says.

The atmosphere in the car grows quiet as Sara dozes off, and Mubashira Apu's eyes are closed, possibly asleep too. But Aleena is still awake, gazing out the window just like before.

A sudden awkwardness settles between us once again. And then she suddenly diverts her eyes from the window to me. "Can I ask you a question?" she asks.

I nod immediately. "Yes"

She pauses, as if grappling with the words lodged in her throat. And then, finally, she asks. "As Sara said, you don't like sharing your clothes with anyone."

"Indeed, I don't," I answer simply, fully aware of the question that is going to come my way. "So for what reason did you lend me your jacket?" she asks, similarly as I had expected.

I grin, knowing exactly what I planned to say.

"Because my future wife doesn't count as 'anyone'."

She just stares at me. Her eyes wide. Then, she jerks her gaze away from me and shifts her focus to the window. She doesn't say anything. Not even a word. The rest of the ride unfolds with her making every possible effort to avoid meeting my eyes.

Once we arrive home, Aleena swiftly exits the car. She's just about to call Sara, but before she can, Mubashira apu and Sara hastily step out of the car and scurry into the house, sticking to each other as if they have some secrets.

Soon after, Aleena steals a glance back at me. But she quickly looks away and walks into the house.

FIFTEEN
ALEENA

I step into the venue and look around at the gorgeous yellow theme that adorned the entire place. It's a sight unlike anything I have ever witnessed in our country because normally holud functions are not celebrated in such a lavish manner.

I wear the yellow matching jhumka with Sara that she has specially chosen for me, perfectly matching my yellow Sharara.

My eyes are immediately drawn to the stage, where Sahil Bhaiya and his beautiful wife, Raisa, stands. I smile, staring at Raisa. She is looking absolutely gorgeous.

In the next moment Sara walks up and whispers something to Raisa. Within seconds, she starts calling me to join them on the stage, most likely for an introduction between me and Raisa.

As I take a step forward, I feel a gentle tug on my bangles. Perplexed, I turn around to see what has caught them, only to find my bangles tangled with someone's sleeve. I look up and realize it's Samir.

His eyebrows raise, and his gaze shifts from his sleeve to me. And then, a smile starts to form on his lips. Memories from the previous day come rushing back, and I try to hide the grin that is trying its utmost to escape.

Samir gently frees my bangles from his sleeve, and a tingling sensation travels through my body. "Thank you," I murmur. He simply nods, his smile lingering for a moment longer before he turns to respond to someone calling him.

"I gotta go," he says before disappearing into the crowd.

I turn around and make my way to the stage, where Sara is patiently waiting for me.

♡

"I wanna eat sandwich"

"Seriously Sara? We are in the middle of dinner. Eat your rice."

"But I miss Sandwich"

"I'll make you one later."

"Love you bestie"

We're all sitting together, enjoying our meal and chatting about various things when Samir's father speaks up. "Tomorrow is my son's wedding, I can't believe how fast time has flown," he says.

"Exactly!" Sara's mom chims in.

"I'm already starting to miss this time. We've had so much fun, and it's hard to imagine going back to the usual routine... boring days ahead," Sara exclaims with a sigh, causing her brothers to chuckle along.

"Yes, Sara, you're absolutely right. Wouldn't it be amazing if we could experience another wedding!?" Mubashira apu adds, a mysterious smile playing on her lips.

"Exactly! Aleena, my bestie, get married soon!" Sara shouts, catching everyone's attention. I freeze mid-chew upon hearing Sara's words. I quickly glance at Samir, who is sitting across from me, his eyes wide with surprise. I nudge Sara but she seems to be enjoying the conversation she initiated.

"Uncle, you should totally start getting things ready for your daughter's wedding," Sara says, glancing at my dad. The next moment my parents laughs. "Hmm, not a bad idea. We can have another wedding celebration together,"

But amidst them, a sudden awkwardness envelops me and Samir.

I absentmindedly twirl my spoon in my plate, trying to focus on my food, but our eyes keep meeting everytime making the ambiance between us even more awkward. The dinner carries on like this, with Samir and I exchanging glances repeatedly.

SIXTEEN

ALEENA

I carefully pick up the necklace and adorn it around my neck. My lips curve into a smile as I gaze at myself through the mirror, overall satisfied with the final look. Turning back at Sara, I call out, "Sara, tell me how do I look?"

My best friend gazes up at me from her phone screen as I twirl around.

"Absolutely gorgeous!!! I love this look!" she exclaims, giving me her full attention.

Sara is already done with her makeup before me, going for a more natural look. I tried to convince her to go to the beauty parlour together, but here we are, doing our own makeup. Even though in this era with the abundance of makeup tutorials and products available, we don't really have to depend on beauty parlours to achieve a flawless look.

It's finally the wedding day. A new member is joining this family, bringing boundless happiness.

"Lets go and check if Sahil bhaiya and others are ready," I say, giving a last check to myself while waiting for Sara to reply. "Yup, let's go," she adds, getting up from her bed and fixing her lehenga.

Just as we're about to leave the room, Mubashira apu enters with a huge smile on her face.

"I'm back!"

"Apu, you look so pretty," I take a moment to observe her from head to toe and Sara does the same.

"Well, I'm not a fan of beauty parlours and makeup, but I must say you look so pretty, Apu!" Sara says.

Mubashira Apu giggles.

"Where is Saad and Eshan Bhaiya?" I ask.

"They are in Sahil's room. Eshan is there to check if Sahil needs any help, and Saad doesn't wanna leave his father, so probably giggling in his father's arms," she replies.

There's a sudden knock on the door, and we look over to check who it is.

My heart skips a beat as I lay eyes on the man standing there.

"Samir bhaiya, you look so handsome!" Sara exclaims while I remain silent, unable to find the right words.

He dons a resplendent, dark green suit looking absolutely flawless. His gaze, fixed upon me, waiting for me to utter something, yet I opt for silence.

"Isn't he looking handsome, Aleena?" Mubashira apu suddenly asks, making me glance at her. "Yeah, he is," I manage to mumble, but I can't bring myself to meet his gaze.

"Um, actually, I came to get all of you downstairs. Sahil bhaiya is ready, and everyone's already settled in the cars," he finally speaks up, but I notice him stealing glances at me, each one weakening me further, sending shivers down my body.

"Yes! Let's go," Sara says, tugging me along.

♡

I wake up from my sleep, feeling the warmth of the morning sun on my face. Gently rubbing my eyes, I gradually open them, allowing the soft morning light to seep in. Grabbing my phone from the nightstand, I groggily check the time and realize it's already 11:00 AM. I don't usually wake up this late, but we all slept late last night, so I didn't realize I ended up sleeping so much.

Glancing at Sara, still lost in her dreams, I decide not to wake her up. I slip out of bed and make my way towards the bathroom to freshen up.

Emerging from the bathroom, I find Sara already awake. I sit on the bed, my eyes still heavy with sleep, and I smile at her adorable morning drowsiness. "Good morning," I cheerfully voice. "Morning," she replies, her voice barely above a whisper, as if she's still caught between the dreams and reality.

Silently, she strolls into the bathroom, while I walk towards the window, pulling back the curtains to invite the sweet sun rays to fill the entire room.

I glance down at my cute bear pajamas, the ones that always bring me comfort during the chilly winter nights. I decide to change my clothes after a little while. With my phone in hand, I settle back onto the bed, propping myself up against the pillows as I scroll through the screen.

Finally, Sara returns, looking all groggy.

"No more sleeping!" I exclaim.

"I still feel so sleepy!" She responds, dropping herself back on the bed.

I place my phone on the bed and gently grab her wrist, urging her to stand up straight. "Don't sleep again!"

"Girls, wake up. It's time to eat something!" Sara's mom walks in.

But just as her eyes land on me, her hand flies to her mouth in surprise. "Aleena! Sweetheart! You look so adorable in those pajamas! You're like a cute little bear!"

"That's her favorite pair, Mom," Sara adds, getting up from the bed all wide awake now.

"Umm, Auntie, I'll go and change!" I say, trying to run away but Sara grabs me back.

"Wait, Aleena! Let me click some pictures of you! Trust me, you really look so adorable!" her mom says, running her fingers over her phone's screen.

"Yes yes mom, she is really looking adorable. Click her pictures please" Sara says, making sure I can't escape as her arm is locked with mine. An arch grin dances on her lips, tempting me to smack her head with my free hand.

"Who is this tiny bear?"

I look over at the door and see Samir standing there, leaning against the doorframe.

NOT THAT LEANING AGAIN SIR!

"Samir bhaiya, look at Aleena. Don't you think she looks adorable?" Sara asks, stealing a glance in his direction. He keeps his arms folded, still leaning, his eyes fixed on me.

"Certainly," he replies with a smile playing on his lips.

But then, his gaze shifts towards his mom, who is busy snapping pictures of me. And in that very moment, I watch him reaching into his pocket and pulling out his phone.

Okay, I know exactly what he's going to do now!

He targets his camera towards me.

I knew it.

"Samir!!! No!! Don't take photos!" I exclaim.

Somehow, I escape from Sara's grip and run towards him, but he's quick enough to slip into the room before I can catch up. "Samir, delete those!" I plead, chasing after him as he maneuvers around the room, his phone clutched tightly in his hand.

"You look seriously adorable!" he teases, standing by the window. He holds his hand high, just out of my reach, as I keep jumping and trying to grab it. "Samir, please give it to me!"

"No!" he responds, dodging my attempts, moving his hand from side to side while I persist, jumping with all my might to grab hold of the phone.

"Samir! Enough! Hand over your phone!" I stand my ground, my voice firm.

His teasing comes to an abrupt halt, and he reluctantly lowers his hand.

"Give me your phone," I voice once again as I extend my hand, beckoning him to pass me his phone.

His face shows this mix of sadness and adorableness as he slowly hands me his phone.

"You were looking absolutely cute in that picture, seriously," he murmurs softly. It's as if he has transformed from the hottest guy leaning against the door just moments ago to the cutest person gazing at me with those innocent eyes.

My heart flutters at this sight.

His gaze is still on me silently asking me not to delete the pictures.

I hand him back the phone. "Okay, but don't you dare show this picture to anyone, alright?"

A triumphant smile spreads across his face, as if he has just reclaimed something incredibly valuable. "I'd rather keep it a secret than let anyone else have the privilege of seeing this precious picture," he murmurs, his eyes fixed on the picture.

"What do you mean?" I ask, although I already have a pretty good idea of what he is trying to say.

He maintains his innocent expression. "I think my words were clear enough for you to hear, right, cutie bear?" He carefully tucks his phone into his pocket, as if my picture is the most precious thing in there.

"Who did you call a bear!" I exclaim, grabbing a pillow from the bed.

"You," he shoots back with that teasing grin. I hurl the pillow towards him, but he effortlessly catches it, showcasing his quick reflexes.

"Get out!" I exclaim, while I try my best not to smile.

"Sure, ma'am!" he says, flashing a smile and soon he exits the room. As his figure disappears I plop onto the bed, to hide my flushed cheeks, all thanks to him!

I step out of the shower and quickly change into a light blue kameez. Just then, Sara rushes into the room. "Come on, Mom wants us to help Raisa bhabi get ready."

We head over to Sahil Bhaiya's room and spot Raisa Bhabi struggling with her sari at the dressing table. "Hey!" I say, catching her attention. "Hi" she responds with a smile before focusing back on her sari.

"Ugh, look how hard they are to wear. That's why I don't like wearing Sari." Sara groans.

"You don't like makeup, you don't like saris... All you care about is your studies!" I tease her.

Raisa, standing nearby, lets out a chuckle, enjoying our banter.

"You're not wrong though. My studies are better than these hard works," Sara responds with a confident toss of her hair.

"Well, we will see it on your wedding day. Who's gonna be there to help you with the Sari?" I add, while assisting

Raisa bhabi with her own Sari.

"You! Of course! You'll come to my in-laws' place and help me get all dressed up." Sara answers and we all burst into laughter.

"Raisa bhabi, I must say you look so beautiful in this Sari," I exclaim.

"Thank you so much for helping. I wasn't understanding how to wear it. Even those YouTube tutorials couldn't help either," she replies, chuckling gently.

"Alright, ready to head downstairs? Some guests are already here to see the new bride!" I say.

Raisa bhabi smiles.

"You must be so excited," I add.

Sara chuckles. "Why wouldn't she be? Her family members are coming in a few hours to visit her."

"That's right though!"

It's a cherished tradition here in Chattogram where the bride's cousins and siblings visit her the day after the wedding.

With Raisa Bhabi, we make our way out of the room.

SEVENTEEN

SAMIR

I walk into my room. The day has been a whirlwind of preparations, but now it's time for me to take a moment for myself. I head straight to the bathroom, eager to wash off all that tiredness and get ready for the Walima that's about to go down.

Stepping into the warm shower, I let the water cascade over me, washing away all that fatigue. The steady rhythm of the water droplets hits my skin and it feels so soothing, like it's rejuvenating my whole body and giving me a fresh burst of energy.

I wrap myself up in a cozy towel, feeling the softness against my skin. I step out of the bathroom and my eyes land on the sleek black suit waiting for me, all classy and sharp. It's perfectly tailored, with a crisp white shirt and a cool bow tie.

After I slip into it, I stand in front of the mirror, running my fingers through my wavy hair, trying to tame the unruly strands. It takes a bit of coaxing, but eventually, I find the perfect balance. I complete my attire with a pair of polished shoes and make my way out of the room. I want everything to be perfect at Sahil bhaiya's walima, so I have to go to the venue early to ensure everything is decorated and arranged properly.

The hall is massive and looks elegant. As I walk in, the silence amplifies the sound of my footsteps. I go around the hall, checking every little detail. I make some small changes here and there, tweaking the decorations until everything is just right.

Soon the guests start filling the hall along with the cameramen. And then my phone buzzes with a call.

Swiftly, I answer it.

"Samir, I'm outside the hall. And the others are here as well. Join us, let's enter together." Sahil bhaiya's voice resonates through the phone.

I hasten outside, but my steps come to a halt as soon as I lay eyes on Aleena. She is wearing a red Sari with her hair cascading over one shoulder with effortless grace, looking extremely gorgeous.

DID MY HEART JUST GIVE A BLACK FLIP?

"Why did you freeze Bhaiya? Come!" Sara's voice echoes through the air, dragging me back to reality.

COME BACK TO YOUR SENSES SAMIR!

Once we walk in together, Sahil bhaiya and Raisa bhabi get settled on the stage, and the hall becomes abuzz with greetings and conversations. But I can't seem to focus on anything else as my eyes linger on Aleena. She's talking to Sara and some of my cousins with a dangerously beautiful smile on her lips.

Samir!! Stay halal! Stay halal! Keep your eyes halal!

I divert my gaze away. But then, I feel someone's presence next to me, and I'm pretty sure who it is. "What's wrong?" Aleena asks, folding her arms. I see this smile on her face, like she knows exactly what she does to me. "Nothing," I reply, tearing my eyes away from her once again. But as I steal another glance at her, I catch her silently smiling at me.

"Why are you smiling?" I ask, trying to stifle my own smile, but eventually, it slips from my lips.

"Now why are you smiling?" she questions.

"I'm not," I reply, my smile still lingering.

"Yes, you smiled. Right now too," she insists, giggling.

My smile gradually fades away and I watch her, silently. She is more than just pretty, she is captivating in every way. Her gaze, her smile, her mere presence has the power to fascinate me.

I'M GOING INSANE!

Her laughter abruptly stops, and she locks her eyes with me. It's like our eyes have their own secret language, saying so much without uttering a single word. I don't know how much longer we will continue gazing into each other's eyes, but all I know is that I never want this moment to end.

"Hey Aleena!" Yasir's voice interrupts us, and we both turn to look at him.

SO, THE MOMENT COMES TO AN END.

I let out an exasperated sigh, knowing exactly what he is up to. "Aleena! Red is definitely your colour!" he says dramatically, hand on his chest.

HERE WE GO AGAIN! HE'S BACK WITH THOSE FLIRTY WORDS!

I notice Aleena giving him this little smile, but it's so obvious that she's not feeling it at all. And that makes me smile, knowing that she is not interested in him at all.

I turn to Yasir and place my hand on his shoulder.

"Why don't you go check if anyone needs anything?"

"Remember, you've got some other tasks to take care of too." He replies, keeping his hand on my shoulder.

HE IS GETTING ON MY NERVES NOW!

However, I still try to stay calm. "Yasir, listen to your elder brother,"

At my words, he smirks, as if he's already prepared for the reply. "Samir Bhaiya, listen to your younger brother," he retorts.

But then, Aleena speaks up, "You both keep deciding who goes where. But for now, I have to go. Enjoy!"

We watch as she walks away, barely holding in her laughter. I glance back at Yasir and exchange eye rolls before we part ways.

EIGHTEEN

ALEENA

I shove my clothes into my suitcase without even folding them properly. The contrast between the happiness of packing your suitcase to start an exciting expedition and the mixed emotions of packing it to go back home is immense. One fills you with excitement, like you can't wait to experience new things, while the other brings a touch of sadness as memories from the whole journey come rushing back.

And I can feel this at this moment. Sahil bhaiya's wedding functions are over. Which means it's my time to go back home, go back to my routines. My dad booked the afternoon flight tomorrow, so I have to start packing my bags now as I don't want to rush at the last moment.

Watching the sunrise, applying henna, sharing stories, laughing under the night sky together, enjoying all the wedding functions—these memories have undoubtedly made this the most incredible time of my life.

"Alee!" Sara storms into the room, her voice brimming with excitement, and I instinctively turn to look at her. Right beside her, Samir enters with a grin on his lips as well. "I'm so happy right now!!" Sara exclaims, taking hold of my hands and twirling me around.

"What happened? What happened?" I ask, trying to figure out the reason behind this sudden excitement. "Remember I applied for the University in California?!?!"

I nod, "I remember."

"Well, guess what? I freaking got in!" She spins me around once again, and in that moment, all the sadness that had been weighing me down dissipates. It's like now I can happily head back home with a big smile on my face.

"Alhamdulillah! I'm so happy for you!!!!" I exclaim, smiling widely. But then my eyes land on Samir and I notice him leaning against the wall and watching us. The smile lingers on his lips. "What's happening here?" Sara's abrupt voice pulls my attention back to her. I see her gazing at my clothes and suitcases.

The happiness is no longer on her face as she acknowledges that I'm leaving soon. "When is the flight? You will at least stay today, right?" she asks, hope in her eyes.

I smile. "Yes, I'll stay today. Our flight is scheduled for tomorrow afternoon."

My attention then shifts towards Samir and now his once cheerful expression has faded. "I have some things to take care of. I gotta go," he states before swiftly exiting the room. My gaze remains fixed on his departing figure until he gradually disappears from my sight, leaving behind a lingering sense of emptiness.

I sit on the bench in the lawn. My eyes are fixated on the vast expanse of the sky above. In the next moment, I feel someone's presence beside me. I turn my head and realize it's Samir, occupying the space next to me. However, he positions himself in such a way that our bodies don't make contact, ensuring that I don't feel uncomfortable.

Our eyes meet briefly before I swiftly break the eye contact and look up at the sky again. "So you're going back tomorrow," he says, his voice barely above a whisper. "Yes," I reply, but I don't look at him. I can feel him nodding his head silently. We stay like this for a few more minutes, silently enjoying the beauty of the blue clear sky.

But then I look back at him.

I study his face, noticing the weight of unexpressed thoughts lingering in his eyes. There's something he wants to say, something he's hesitant to share. It's as if each time he tries to open up, his words get caught in his throat.

He looks away.

I remain silent, waiting for him to eventually speak it out. Abruptly, his eyes land on me, and I can sense that he's ready to voice his words. "It feels like I've gotten used to you," he confesses, his voice trembling ever so slightly.

My heart skips a beat.

I find myself at a loss for words. I want to respond, to let him know how I feel, but the right words? The right words elude me. The weight of his gaze intensifies, as if he's searching for a response, any response, from me. But all I can do is remain silent, my mind racing with thoughts and emotions that I can't put into words.

"I gotta go. I've got some things to pack," I somehow manage to voice, and about to get off the bench when his abrupt voice stops me. "Stay for a few more minutes. Please."

I look back at him. His eyes... They're silently pleading with me, telling me to stay by his side.

I sit back next to him, my lips searching for words. "My semester exams are starting soon. I'll get busy preparing for my exams as soon as I reach home. You, Sara, are going back to the US. Everyone will be chasing their dreams and goals." I say.

He just hums in response.

"Where's that awesome smile of Mr. Samir Zafar?" I tease, hoping to bring it out. I know that with a little effort, I can make him smile.

As I gaze into his eyes, a glimmer of amusement appears, and a slight smile begins to form on his lips.

"You think my smile is something special?" he asks, raising an eyebrow.

"Without any doubts, YES," my words make him smile even wider this time. "You've got these killer dimples!" I add.

We carry on our conversation for a few more minutes until I realize it's time for me to go back inside.

"I really gotta go now," I say, slowly getting up. This time he doesn't stop me.

I quickly dash back into the house, feeling his gaze follow me until I disappear from his sight.

NINETEEN

ALEENA

"I'll miss you" I wrap my arms around my best friend, giving her a tight squeeze. We're at the airport with Sara and Samir dropping us off. I've already said goodbye to their family back home, and honestly, I'm really gonna miss all of them. While Sara talks to my parents, I turn to Samir, standing right next to me. We both stand in silence, not saying a word.

"I have to go now." I say and look up at him, hoping he'll say something, but he simply nods. I linger for a moment, still waiting, but then, I suddenly hear my parent's voices from behind.

I steal one last glance in his direction and take a step forward with my parents. The distance between us grows, yet I can still feel his intense gaze fixated on me. I can't resist the urge, so I turn my head to steal another look at him. There he stands, his eyes saying so much, as if they're desperately yearning to convey something to me. As if he wants to bridge the gap between us, to come running towards me and pour his heart out.

Taking one last lingering glance at him and Sara, I walk away, heading towards the plane.

NEXT DAY
Ringing
Ringing
Ringing

My eyes lingers on my phone screen as I wait for Sara to pick up the call. And then her face pops up.

"Good Morning bestie!" I exclaim.

"Good morning, Aleena! I miss you a lot" she pouts.

"I miss you too."

"By the way, have you started packing yet?" I inquire.

"Not yet. Seriously, I brought my entire closet from the US, and now I'm stuck deciding what to pack and what to leave behind!" she says, letting out a frustrated sigh.

"Sara, you've got my AirPods again, haven't you?" an all-too-familiar voice interrupts us abruptly.

"Who are you talking to?" he asks.

"It's Aleena," Sara responds.

In the blink of an eye, he snatches the phone from her grasp, and our eyes meet through the screen. A heavy silence envelops me, leaving me momentarily speechless and unsure of what to say.

"Samir bhaiya, what's wrong with you!?" Sara's voice echoes.

"I just wanted to ask her if she had reached home safely" Samir's response comes swiftly and I can feel Sara letting out a sigh. "Bhaiya, I've already told you multiple times yesterday that she reached her home without any issues."

But it seems that he's got some other plans in mind. He dashes out of Sara's room, vanishing into his own, leaving me completely speechless.

"What are you doing?!" I blurt out.

But what surprises me even more is that Sara doesn't even bother calling out to her brother to get her phone back.

Samir just stars at me, all quiet and with this little smile playing on his lips.

"First you snatched my bestie's phone, and now you're smiling at me like a creep. What's going on Mr Samir Zafar?" I ask, in an attempt to tease him.

"I wanted to talk to you"

"So you could've called me from your own phone"

"I don't have your number"

"You didn't ask for my number!

"I wanted you to give me your number yourself"

His words render me utterly speechless.

I remain silent, my breath catches in my chest, as his words washes over me like a gentle caress. "But isn't it the same thing? You could've simply asked for my number" I say, my voice barely above a whisper.

"No, Aleena, it is definitely not the same. I don't wanna be like those typical guys, just asking for your number with that intention. I want you to feel comfortable and safe before you decide to share your number with me." he replies, with a soft shake of his head.

My heart goes all aflutter like a delicate butterfly.

And I'm at a loss for words once again.

HE IS SO SPECIAL!

TWENTY
ALEENA

Two months later

I plop down onto my cozy bed, feeling the weight of exhaustion settling in. These past two months have been an absolute rollercoaster for me, filled with endless studying and the stress of my semester final exams. It feels like time has flown by in a blur, leaving me with little room to breathe.

And then there is Sara, who has already started her new journey in California. The distance between us, coupled with the time difference again. We used to make sure we have time for each other every single day, but now that we're both more serious and busy with our studies, it's become a bit tougher. Our daily chats turn into weekly catch-ups, and although it isn't the same, we've made a pact to keep our bond alive, no matter what.

Honestly, I can't blame Sara either. Moving to a new place all by herself, tackling studies, and taking charge of her own schedule—it's not an easy feat for her either. But I'm happy that she's handling it with so much courage and strength.

I stare at the ceiling. It's crazy how time flies. Days turn into weeks, weeks turn into months, and it feels like everyone I know is getting caught up in their own things. The once carefree days of endless laughter and shared moments are slowly giving way to the pursuit of individual ambitions.

I get off my bed, grab my hair clip, and twist my hair up into a bun, securing it with the hair clip. As I step out of my room, I notice some preparations happening around the house. I stroll into the kitchen and spot my mom. "What's happening, Mom? Any guests dropping by?"

"I was just about to come and tell you to get ready. There's a family coming to meet you for a potential marriage match." my mom replies, her hands busy preparing food.

My mind goes blank.

My body freezes.

"How could you make such a decision without consulting me first?" My voice tinges with frustration, and tears threaten to spill from my eyes.

This time my mom turns to face me. "Sweetheart, we are not trying to force you into anything. Just give him a chance, spend some time with him, and who knows, you might end up liking the idea of marriage." Her words hang in the air, leaving me at a loss for words.

I can't even put into words how unbelievably awful I feel right now. My heart is pounding with fear, and then out of nowhere, thoughts of Samir just pop into my head. Why is he occupying my thoughts at a time like this?

Despite the chaos of emotions, one thing is clear - I am deeply unhappy with the situation unfolding before me.

"And do you even know who they are?" my mom asks but honestly, I'm totally not in the mood to continue the conversation. I don't give a single care about who they really are at this point. "I don't want to know." I snap back and I storm out of the kitchen.

I close the door in my room, feeling a heavy sigh escape my lips. Everything feels so confusing, and I'm not sure what to do. They want me to meet this family for marriage, and I'm not happy about it. But I don't want to let my parents down either. I saw the excitement on my mom's face when she was getting everything ready, and perhaps my dad is happy too.

I sit down on my bed, taking a deep breath, trying to calm myself. "My parents won't force me... It's just a meeting... Nothing more," I remind myself, even though tears start welling up in my eyes.

"Aleena, get ready fast!" I hear my mom from the kitchen. I gather myself and push myself up. "Calm down, Aleena. It's just a meeting. Calm down," I whisper to myself as I make my way to the closet, picking out a simple kameez. The emotions inside me are all jumbled up. Do all the girls feel like this in similar situations?

I grab the comb from the dressing table and gently run it through my hair, trying to stay calm. I don't feel like putting on any makeup, so I decide to go natural.

As I finish getting ready, I steal one last glance in the mirror. My cheeks are still flushed from the tears, a tangible sign of the battle raging within me. But I know I have to put on a brave face. It's not just about me; it's about the hopes and dreams my parents have for me.

I walk out of my room and catch sight of my Mom and Dad eagerly awaiting my presence. I muster a smile, but my attention quickly shifts to the sound of the doorbell, capturing their attention as well.

"Let me go and open it!" my mom exclaims, as she hurriedly makes her way towards the main door.

As I gaze at the figures standing before me, my eyes widen.

It's Samir, accompanied by his parents, and alongside them is Sahil bhaiya and his wife Raisa. The realization hits me like a lightning bolt.

It's Samir.

IT'S HIM!

As our eyes meet, I notice the unmistakable spark of excitement and joy dancing within his gaze. It's as if his eyes are a mirror, reflecting the same emotions that swirl within my own heart. I don't know how I can decipher his every emotion through his eyes. It's like his eyes are a window into his mind, allowing me to understand what's going on inside him without any words being spoken.

As I greet everyone, Samir's mom approaches me, wrapping me in her warm and loving embrace. "My sweetheart, you look absolutely beautiful. I'm so happy that you are going to be my daughter-in-law," she says, bringing a smile to my face.

I turn my head to look at Samir, and there it is—a gentle smile playing on his lips, silently affirming his happiness.

Wait, is this really happening or am I in some crazy dream?

Should I actually pinch myself to make sure?

Even if it's all a dream, I don't wanna wake up from it!

No No No!

This is not a dream!

IT'S REAL!

TWENTY-ONE
SAMIR

I stand in front of the door with my family by my side. My hands intertwined, my heart racing, and there's a dangerously twisting sensation deep inside me.

I'm excited.

Restless.

Going absolutely crazy.

Just to catch a glimpse of her.

The door swings open and her mom appears. I tilt my head slightly behind her and there she stands, staring at us with eyes wide open. Whatever twisted, intense feeling that had consumed me just moments ago suddenly fades away.

My heart instantly finds peace seeing her right before my eyes.

Once we settle ourselves in the drawing room suddenly, Aleena's dad catches our attention. "I still remember that day when Sara requested Aleena to get married quickly. I never could have imagined her wish would come true so soon."

My dad chuckles. "Well, imagine how happy our daughter would be if she was here with us."

Everyone continues their conversations but their words slowly become distant whispers, and all I can see is her. She catches my eye, then quickly looks away, but then she steals another glance at me, silently begging me to stop staring. I absolutely love how her cheeks turn the most adorable shade of red every time I look at her.

"Alright, so I know I've already mentioned it, but let me reiterate. We've come here with a marriage proposal for Aleena, regarding my son, Samir," my mom announces abruptly.

"Samir, Aleena, if you both want, you can have some time alone to talk and decide what you truly want. It's a huge decision, after all," Aleena's mom suggests.

Aleena shoots me a quick glance and I can sense she is waiting for my response. I get up from my seat and stride towards her. "Shall we?" I ask, with a grin. She returns the smile, and together we make our way to the poolside behind her house. As we walk, I catch Aleena stealing glances at me, which brings a smile to my face. She eventually tears her eyes away and looks towards the pool.

There's a moment of silence before Aleena speaks up. "Did you have any idea about this?" she asks.

I meet her gaze and shake my head. "No way. It was just as surprising for me too. I had no clue. Let me tell you-"

～

I step into my room and plop my tired body onto my bed, letting out a sigh of exhaustion. It has been a hectic day at the office, after all.

"Samir, get up. I have something important to discuss with you," My mom rushes into my room with a huge smile on her face.

Sitting up, I glance at her, confused. "What's wrong, mom?" I ask. She places herself next to me on the bed. "Look, you are already settled. Everything is going well, and you're at an age where you could find your perfect match and start a beautiful life together."

Her words clearly convey her intentions. But I feel a piercing ache in my heart. I realize that the things I've been wanting to tell my mom for a while now, I just have to express them right now.

I gently take her hands in mine. "Mom, I know how excited you are for my marriage. I know... but... mom- I'm sorry. I'm really, really sorry. I never want to hurt you, I never can, but there is someone else I want in my life... I really can't express how all of this happened. I mean....I don't know, but all I know now is I can't imagine any other woman as my wife except her."

I take a moment to stare at her, fear filling my chest, hoping for understanding. Her eyes hold a blend of sadness and surprise. "Who is she?" she asks gently. With a slight tilt of my head, I take a deep breath, and meet her gaze once again. "Aleena."

Her expression quickly changes, and she releases her hand from mine to grab her phone, which is conveniently placed nearby. And then she turns the phone toward me. "She's the one I was talking about... for your marriage."

My eyes widen in surprise as I see Aleena's face in the picture. I turn back to my mom and pull her into a tight embrace. "No way, mom! It was her all along! I can't believe it!"

I feel her body shaking with laughter against mine. "Aleena is such a wonderful girl. I've liked her from the very beginning, and I've always hoped she'd become my daughter-in-law."

~

I finish speaking, my eyes still on Aleena. She stands there, motionless, her eyes reflecting her surprise. Slowly, I reach into my pocket, retrieving a small box. Her eyes shift to the box and then back to me.

I turn towards her completely and take a deep breath. "I know you're aware of my feelings for you. I've never directly confessed before, but now, I can't bear to wait any longer."

With trembling hands, I open the box, revealing a dazzling ring that glistens under the moon's gentle glow. "Aleena, will you give me the chance to love you forever?"

She gazes at the ring.

Gradually, her eyes meet mine, and she presses her lips together, restraining the tears that yearn to cascade down her cheeks.

In an instant, a sudden cheer fills the air, and we notice the beaming faces of our families. My mom starts capturing the memory on her phone, while Sara joins in through FaceTime. Aleena's parents, with their reassuring gazes, convey their approval.

I turn my attention back to Aleena, and she remains stunned, struggling to process everything. Finally, her focus returns to me, and a smile gradually illuminates her face.

"Aleena,"

"Will you marry me?"

Tears of happiness stream down her cheeks. Her smile widens, and she gently reaches out her hand toward me. "Yes, Samir, I will marry you. With all my heart."

I gently slide the ring onto her finger, feeling a mix of excitement and nervousness. Just then, her mom rushes over, holding another ring box. Aleena takes the ring and meets my gaze. I extend my hand, and she carefully places the ring on my finger, eliciting a chorus of cheers and applause from our family.

As our families engage in their own conversations, Aleena and I stand together, observing them. I steal a glance at Aleena, as she reaches out her hand towards me. "Give me your phone" she says, smiling slightly. Surprised, I raise an eyebrow and swiftly retrieve my phone from my pocket, handing it to her.

I watch as she dials her number on my phone and then hands it back to me. "Finally!" I exclaim, making her giggle. I quickly type something and turn the phone screen toward her, hoping she'll see it.

Cute Bear

"Bear? Again? Don't call me that, Samir,"

"No, this name is cute."

"It's not."

"It is"

TWENTY-TWO
ALEENA

Year 2021

I sit in front of the mirror, feeling all anxious and excited at the same time. My heart's pounding like crazy. The moment I have been waiting for is just half an hour away.

Today is my Akht.

And I'm officially becoming his wife.

The reason I'm getting married after two years is because I wanted to pursue my studies before diving into married life. Lucky for me, Samir and his family have been incredibly supportive. Their love and understanding have given me the confidence to step into the new chapter of my life.

Over the past two years, Samir and I have become even closer. We've learned so much about each other's likes and dislikes. Our understanding of one another has grown stronger. It feels like we're fully prepared to start this new journey together, hand in hand.

As I look at my reflection, a mix of emotions swirl within me. My eyes travel to the beautiful sari I've chosen for this special day. The soft fabric drapes gracefully around me, and a veil adorns my head. The simple jewelry I wear perfectly complements the overall look.

It's just perfect.

But honestly, there is something that makes me feel a bit sad inside.

Sara.

The fact that she can't make it from the US due to unforeseen circumstances really hits me deep. It feels like a vital piece of my happiness puzzle is missing, and no matter how much I try to fill that void, it remains unfulfilled without her presence.

"SURPRISE"

A gentle voice comes from the doorway. My eyes widen, realizing who the person is.

"Sara!"

There she is, standing at my door, all dressed up for my Akht. A big smile spreads across her face. I jump out of my chair and rush over to her, pulling her into a tight hug. "You scared me so bad with this surprise! I was almost in tears!" I say, feeling her body vibrate against mine as she chuckles.

"I didn't know you would find this surprise scary" she responds and her voice remains gentle. Pulling away she gazes at me from head to toe. "You are looking so pretty MashaAllah" I smile. "So as you. You've gotten much prettier!"

She shakes her head while we both laugh together. "But why are you here? You should be with Samir. He's your brother, before I'm your bestie," I say, sounding concerned.

"No worries, I talked to him. He's got Sahil bhaiya, and we have plenty of cousins too. But you don't have any siblings or too many cousins. Plus, the most important thing is that I want to be by my bestie's side on this special day."

"So today, I'm on the bride's side." Her gentle voice fills me with warmth, wrapping me in a comforting embrace.

"Sara, I love you so much!"

"Love you more"

"By the way, you should get emotional! Your bestie is getting married today!" I exclaim with an exaggerated sigh. "Should I really get all teary-eyed? 'Cause honestly, I ain't feeling it," she replies, raising an eyebrow.

"Seriously! You know I ain't asking you to shed real tears. Where's my dramatic Sara? Bring her back!" I demand.

She chuckles. "Uh.. Maybe gone"

"I just ain't feeling the need for all that drama," she adds.

Ever since Sara moved to California, I notice a change in her demeanor. She has gotten more serious and reserved, like a whole different person. It's like I hardly recognize her now. Well, people change, and maybe she is going through some changes too. But no matter what, I'll always be there to support her.

We turn our eyes towards the door, and there stand my mom and dad, filling the room with warmth. They walk toward me, enveloping me in a gentle hug. When we pull apart, I see a tear rolling down my dad's cheek.

"I can't believe our little girl is getting married today," my mom whispers, her eyes glistening with tears.

"You look so beautiful," my dad says. Tears well up in my eyes, blurring my vision. Just as the emotions threaten to overwhelm us, my aunt steps in, breaking the tender moment. "Time to go, honey. Samir and his family are already at the venue," she says.

I take a deep breath and nod. Together, we make our way to the venue.

We wanted the decorations to be simple, with light-colored flowers and minimal adornments. As I walk further and take in the surroundings, I smile. It's exactly what I had envisioned.

The sunlight pours in, enveloping everything in its warm embrace. But when I see the man sitting in front me, my heart skips a beat. It's Samir, looking absolutely stunning in his groom's attire. A wide smile spreads across my face, but he seems lost in his own thoughts, his gaze fixed on his fiddling fingers. I can sense the nervousness radiating from him.

With Sara, my mom, my dad, and my relatives surrounding me I take a step forward. I ascend the stage and take my place in front of him. There is a veil between us, keeping us from seeing each other.

I adjust the delicate veil that drapes over my head, my hand trembling with excitement.

The moment has arrived.

Suddenly, The Kazi's voice cuts through the air, asking if I will accept Samir as my husband. My heart races, and behind me, I feel the reassuring presence of Sara and my parents, silently cheering me on. I take a deep breath, summoning all my courage, and speak the word that will bind us together.

The Kazi turns to Samir, asking him the same question. I hold my breath, waiting for his answer. And then, I hear him say the same one syllable. A smile blooms on my lips, mirroring the happiness in my heart.

We continue with the rest of the rituals, and finally, the long-awaited moment arrives - we are married.

Everyone cheers as the veil that stands between us is lifted, revealing our faces to one another.

Samir approaches me, slowly lifting the veil to reveal my face. As our eyes meet, he falls silent, his gaze filled with love. A smile slowly forms on my lips. Tears start to well up in his eyes, shining with emotions he can't put into words.

"MashaAllah." He whispers.

We both stand up, unable to take our eyes off each other. He leans in to plant a gentle kiss on my forehead.

At this moment I just know that I am his and he is mine.

"You look incredibly beautiful, my love," he whispers, sending a wave of warmth through my body.

"And you look incredibly handsome," I reply, sharing a chuckle with him.

His hand slowly reaches out toward me. I smile widely as I place my hand in his, feeling the comforting warmth of his touch enveloping me. It's our first time holding hands, and it feels incredibly special. His hand, strong and comforting, wraps around mine, giving me a sense of security I've never felt before. It's like all my worries and fears just fade away, replaced by this comforting feeling that he'll be there, holding my hand, for the rest of my life.

TWENTY-THREE
ALEENA

I'm sitting in the drawing room, surrounded by friends and relatives. The house is aglow with wedding preparations, just like Sahil's bhaiya's wedding. And now, I can't believe it's my turn. Samir and his family are staying here in Dhaka. They've got accommodation sorted since they already have an apartment in the city.

I glance at the henna artist, whose nimble fingers dance gracefully across my hands, adorning them with beautiful henna designs. "This is so pretty," I say, staring at the henna she's applying on my hand.

She smiles in response.

Suddenly, Sara's voice diverts my attention. "Make sure to hide Samir bhaiya's name in the henna. We'll make him search for it."

In the next moment, everyone starts agreeing with Sara, urging the henna artist to hide his name perfectly.

She smiles. "Don't worry. I'll hide his name in the designs so well that it will be hard for him to find it."

I gaze at my phone placed beside me as the familiar ringtone fills the room. A smile spreads across my face when I see Samir's face illuminating my phone screen with a video call. But just as my hand reaches out to grab the phone, another hand swiftly swoops in and snatches it away from me. I look up and notice Mubashira apu. This time, my smile widens even more.

"Mubashira apu, when did you come?"

I jump up from my seat and approach her, ready to envelop her in a tight embrace, but she stops me midway, her gaze fixed on my henna. "You don't want to smudge these beautiful designs, do you?'"

We smile at each other and settle back on the sofa. "I had to come and see how the bride is doing. Plus, the bride's best friend is here, so I couldn't resist," Mubashira apu says, smiling at me and Sara.

We hear the phone ring again and this time she picks it up.

"Who stole my wife's phone?" Samir's voice booms through the speakers, as he catches Mubashira apu on the screen instead of me.

"When did you drive there, Apu?" Samir asks.

"Secret, I ain't telling you" Mubashira Apu quips.

"Then why are you still holding the phone? Hand it back to my wife."

I can see Mubashira Apu bursting into giggles. "Alright, here you go. Your husband is absolutely desperate to talk to you"

Mubashira Apu hands me back my phone, and there it is, his smiling face lighting up the screen. "Samir, I'll talk to you later. I'm kind of busy now"

"Seriously? We haven't even had a chance to talk yet."

"I promise, I'll give you a call later."

"Fine" he replies, a hint of disappointment in his voice before we end the call.

♡

Sara is staying over at my place tonight. She is currently with my mom to check out all the wedding stuff my mom has bought and my mom won't let her leave until she shows her every single thing! She absolutely loves Sara.

And about Mubashira apu, she took off because her husband called. Apparently, their son was crying and needed her.

I head to my room and shut the door behind me. But as I glance beside me, I nearly jump out. "Samir! What are you doing here!?" I whisper, spotting him leaning against the wall, staring right at me. "What if someone saw you? And why are you here this late!?"

He doesn't say a word, just gazes at me, flaunting those irresistible dimples on his cheeks.

"Say something!" I urge him, wanting to break his silence.

"I wanted to see you," he responds, still holding his position.

"You could've just called me! A facetime?"

"As if you're talking to me. You seem so busy." he retorts, rolling his eyes.

"What's with that face?" I ask.

"What response do you expect to get from me after you ignored me?" He snaps back.

"I never ignored you," I defend myself.

"You did, basically," he insists.

"I was applying henna, so I couldn't talk," I explain.

This time, he remains silent but just stares at me.

I look away, trying to hold back my smile.

"Don't hold it in. Let it out. I've come all this way at this hour just to see that," he replies, causing a slight giggle to well up within me. "I'm observing you. You've become so flirty and cheesy since we got married."

"What do you mean? I've always been like this," He stands up straight.

I cross my arms. "Well, I never saw this side of you before we got married."

He tucks his hands into his pockets. "That's because I believe in 'Stay Halal until you make it halal.'"

A sudden silence envelopes us.

But then he takes a step forward.

I watch as he slowly moves nearer to me, causing me to instinctively take a step back, knowing that I'll soon be pressed against the wall behind me. And the next moment I find myself pinned against the wall by his strong hands firmly grasping my waist. My hands rest lazily on either side of me, not even making an effort to push him away.

I can feel the touch of his hand on my waist.

Does that mean he can feel the butterflies fluttering in my stomach?

Even if he doesn't, I still want him to know, I want him to know the immensely intoxicating effect he has on me.

He leans in closer, so close that I can feel his warm breath against my skin.

"Don't ignore me again," he whispers.

OKAY, THE BUTTERFLIES INSIDE ME ARE GOING ABSOLUTELY WILD!

"I told you, I never ignored you. I was just busy getting the henna done," I manage to blurt out. One of his hands releases its firm grip on my waist and instead takes hold of my hand. His eyes focused on the designs on my hand, searching until he spots something. "They should've hidden the name better. It was way too easy to find."

My eyes widen, and I quickly pull my hand away from his. "How did you find your name so quickly?"

He just flashes a proud smile in response.

"You have no idea how excited everyone is for the mehedi ceremony tomorrow, just to see you find the name," I say, watching him chuckle. But then, he leans in closer, and that smile? I don't think he even knows what it means right now.

"You're my bride, and that name on your hand is mine too. Don't you think you should just focus on how excited I got after seeing it?" His whisper against my skin is the most dangerously addictive thing I've ever discovered.

THIS MAN CAN GO FROM BEING THE CUTEST TO THE HOTTEST IN A SPLIT SECOND!

"What's going on Samir Zafar? You are acting different today"

"Why? Don't you like it?"

"It was pretty dramatic but I- wait- speaking of which, how did you manage to sneak in here!?"

His expression goes all blank, almost as if he expected something else instead of the sudden question. "I have my own ways"

Before I can inquire further, a sudden knock on the door startles me. "Aleena, open the door. It's me," Sara calls out from the other side.

I give Samir a quick look, then shift my gaze towards the door, and finally back to Him. "Hide!" I gently push him away, my voice barely audible.

"But why should I hide? I'm your husband." he protests.

"Because you didn't just walk in like a normal person. You sneaked in somehow, and if my bestie sees you here, it's gonna be so awkward!" I start searching the room frantically, trying to find a good hiding spot.

"Well, I guess you're right." he agrees, scratching the back of his neck.

I manage to hide Samir and make my way to the door, opening it just in time. "What took you so long?" Sara exclaims as she enters the room. I give her an awkward smile, not knowing what to answer. She plops down on my bed, gazing up at the ceiling. "Tomorrow's your mehedi ceremony, then the holud, then the wedding ceremony, and then the walima, and finally, you'll be staying with us"

I chuckle in response, joining her on the bed.

But suddenly, a soft shuffling sound emanates from the corner where Samir is hiding. Sara's eyes dart in that direction, and my heart leaps into my throat, desperately hoping she doesn't pay it too much attention. "What's over there?" she asks. I let out an awkward chuckle. "Uh, haha, maybe a rat."

"Rat? She turns over, looking at me, resting her head on her palm. "Speaking of which, you know Samir Bhaiya is absolutely terrified of rats. We have so many funny stories about him and his encounters with those rats"

I burst into laughter, joining in with hers. "No way!"

"I remember this one time when he was in 8th grade, he ended up sleeping with mom because he spotted a rat in his room."

My laughter mingles with hers but then it slowly fades away. I bite my lip, unsure of what to do as Samir's presence in the room makes it certain that he heard her too. I just hope he won't come out and expose himself in front of Sara.

"How can you just make fun of your brother like that!?" Samir walks out, raising his eyebrows at his sister.

Boom! The exact thing I was afraid of has happened.

Sara stands up from the bed, arms crossed, and shoots her brother an unbothered look. "Hi Bhaiya"

Samir pauses and gives me a quick look, then turns his attention back to his sister. "Um…hey," he stammers.

"I knew this would get you to walk out in front of me." Sara says, wearing a proud expression.

"Wait, you knew he was here?" I ask, just as puzzled as Samir.

"Yup! I saw him sneaking in."

"Anyways, since you're here, let's do something exciting," Sara adds.

"Like what?" I ask.

"How about a long drive?" Samir suggests and I glance over at him.

"Let's go on a long drive, the three of us." he adds.

"Perfect" Sara exclaims. "Let's go. I'll go grab my hijab"

"Wait, Sara and I can get out easily, but what about you?" I ask.

I observe Samir as he strides towards the bed and settles on its edge, stealing a glance at his sister.

"When you've got an awesome sister like me, there's no need to stress. I'll help you to get outta here," Sara says, wrapping the hijab around her head.

I giggle. "All set then! Let's go!"

TWENTY-FOUR
ALEENA

The sun is going down, casting a beautiful golden glow all over my house's lawn. And honestly, the holud decorations are on point. The colors are just popping everywhere, creating this super vibrant and lively atmosphere. My lawn may not be as big as Samir's, but it's still spacious enough to fit everyone.

I sat with Samir right beside me, surrounded by all our loved ones. The air is filled with laughter, chats, and the mouthwatering smell of delicious Bengali foods.

I quickly scan the crowd, searching for familiar faces. And there she is, my mom, making her way towards me, holding a bowl of holud in her hands. Holud is basically Turmeric Paste.

With a warm smile, my mom takes a pinch of Turmeric paste and gently applies it to Samir's and my cheeks.

And then Sara comes. She dips her fingers into the Turmeric paste and applies the bright yellow paste on our cheeks.

Soon others join in.

I look at the yellow paste and then glance at Samir. In a swift Motion I grab a handful of Turmeric paste and smear it on Samir's cheeks, creating bright yellow streaks that stand out against his skin.

His eyes widens. "Aleena Noor!"

I let out a giggle, which only encourages him to retaliate in the best way possible. He takes a good deal of Turmeric paste and smudges it on my cheeks, creating a matching set of yellow streaks. This time, it's his turn to laugh at me.

In the next moment, laughter and cheers erupt around us. "Okay, enough. Let's wrap up the fun. Aleena, take Samir inside and help him clean off the Turmeric paste," my mom says, accompanied by a slight chuckle.

We walk into my house and I grab a bowl of water and a clean towel. Stepping into my room, I plop the bowl of water on my dressing table. "Samir, you can sit there. Let me wipe my face real quick," I tell him, motioning towards the couch tucked in the corner of my room.

I dip the small towel into the water, making sure to squeeze it just right, letting the extra droplets drip back into the bowl. With a gentle touch, I press the cool fabric against my cheeks, feeling the remnants of the Turmeric Paste getting wiped away, revealing my natural face.

As I finish wiping my cheeks, I swiftly dry my hands with a soft tissue while I can sense his unwavering gaze upon me. I look back at him, finding him leaning back on the couch, arms folded, a smile playing on his lips.

"What are you looking at?" I ask.

"My beautiful wife," he smoothly replies, making my cheeks turn red.

"Don't distract me, Samir. I need to focus," I say, but he just lets those adorable dimples linger on his cheeks.

"You've stolen all my attention, and now you're telling me not to distract you? That's not fair,"

His words elicit a giggle from deep within me, and I catch a glimpse of him giggling along with me. I close the distance between us, and plop myself next to him.

"Samir, seriously, you gotta stop now!" I say, pressing my hand on his mouth while I try my best to stifle my laughter.

But then I feel the warmth of his lips beneath my palm, and a sudden shiver runs through me. I quickly pull my hand away, and our laughter fades. I can sense him silently observing me. Clearing my throat, I pick up the bowl, change the water, and return to his side. "Here, take this and remove the paste from your face."

But his arms remain folded and he stares at me, "I don't know how to do that. Can you help me, my cute bear?"

I can still spot the dimples on his cheeks.

I give him a brief stare, then place the bowl on the small table in front of the couch and smack his arm. "There you go again, using that nickname,"

He chuckles. "But my cute bear, it suits you so well. I'll never stop calling you that."

"Whatever."

I slide in beside him, grabbing the towel from the bowl. With a gentle squeeze, I start wiping off the Turmeric Paste from his cheeks.

I shuffle a bit nearer, aiming for a thorough cleaning. But as our eyes meet, something shifts. His intense gaze carries no trace of a smile. "You've come so close, Aleena," he murmurs, his eyes drifting down to my lips.

And that's when it hits me - we are sitting so close. So close that anything can happen at any moment.

I can feel his hot breath against my lips, my body, every inch of me.

He gets even closer, our noses touching just right, and I feel a tingling sensation throughout me. My hand instinctively moves away, and the towel slips from my grasp, landing on the ground.

I feel my whole body going numb under his intense stare, and I can't even find the energy to grab the towel and put it back in the bowl.

"What are you doing?" I can hear my voice trembling.

But he doesn't say a word.

I watch him inching closer and closer and closer, until finally our lips meet.

Wait, he is kissing me!?

Samir Zafar is kissing me!?

I never knew a kiss could be this special until now. I place my hands on his chest and gently push him away, breaking our kiss. "Someone might see us," I whisper, but his eyes remain fixated on my lips, as if my words just bounce off him.

"'Samir!" I call out again.

"I'm kissing my wife, not anyone else," he whispers, and presses his lips against mine once again.

He gently tucks a strand of hair behind my ear, then leans in and deepens the kiss. I can feel a warm sensation filling my chest.

I close my eyes.

His lips...

Against mine.

I'm going insane!

I gently push him away, my breaths escaping rapidly.

I quickly clean off the remaining Turmeric Paste from his face and get off the couch, while he does the same.

"L-et's g-o," I say, my voice trembling slightly. I can feel his intense gaze on me, making millions of butterflies dance in my stomach. I glance back at him for a moment, then quickly look away again.

But he pulls me back into his arms and kisses me once again.

"I'm so obsessed....With you" he whispers against my lips.

"Let's go, Samir."

He kisses me.

"Sami-"

Another kiss interrupts my words.

"Samir, stop now!" I say, this time giggling.

Just as I notice a lipstick mark on his lips, I swiftly brush it away with my thumb.

"Look what you've done. You stole all my lipstick"

His smile mirrors mine. I glance back in the mirror, fix my lipstick and grab his hand. "Come on, let's go,"

TWENTY-FIVE
SAMIR

I sit in the car, waiting for Aleena, outside the venue. My heart is pounding with excitement. We chose Chattogram for our wedding ceremony to make things easier for both the families. I have a huge family, while Aleena, on the other hand, doesn't have many relatives. So we decided to have the wedding ceremony in the city where our family can easily gather.

I glance at my watch and then shift my gaze back outside the window, hoping to catch a glimpse of her arrival.

Suddenly, the sound of a car horn pierces the air.

"She is here" I whisper.

With Sahil and Eshan Bhaiya by my side, I step out of the car.

The door swings open and there she stands. Her eyes sparkles with excitement, mirroring the happiness that light up my own face. She is wearing a red lehenga, looking so pretty. It reminds me of the day of Sahil bhaiya's walima, when she adorned herself in that gorgeous red sari. But today, she is even more resplendent in this red lehenga.

Red is definitely her color.

I walk up to her, closing the distance between us. "MashaAllah. You look absolutely gorgeous." I whisper.

She raises her eyebrows proudly. "Well, I'm Samir Zafar's bride, after all"

I smile.

"Yes, my bride"

TWENTY-SIX
ALEENA

I step into the bedroom with Samir and my gaze immediately falls upon the bed. Memories of that day rushes back, causing a smile to grace my lips. "What are you looking at?" Samir inquires, his voice drawing closer as he approaches me.

"That day. I remember it so vividly," I reply, settling onto the bed and allowing a giggle to escape my throat. "I had innocently mistaken this room for the guest room and ended up lying down right here. It was quite embarrassing."

"I bet you've been planning ever since to claim this bed as your own, huh?" He teases, raising an eyebrow.

"Hahaha, that's so funny," I jest. But then, a smirk appears on my lips. "Well, I didn't have high hopes back then. But I didn't know that someone was head over heels for me and would eventually propose," I say, subtly referring to him.

I watch him lean closer to me. "That's true, though," he whispers. "Speaking of which, you never hit me up with an answer that day. But you've to answer me right now. So... Is the bed comfortable?" he whispers, his hot breath caressing my lips as our noses brush against each other.

I place my hands on either side of me on the bed and start moving them in slow, gentle circles while keeping our eye contact unbroken. "Yes, way more comfier than I expected. I liked it,"

A slight smirk forms at the corner of my lips as I keep going, my fingers reaching the back of his neck, pulling him in closer. Our lips almost touch, teasingly close. His breath gets all shaky, making my smirk grow wider.

Just as he's about to engulf my lips, I push him away and soon a giggle crawls up my throat.

"First you turned me on with your 'those' moves and now giggling like a cute baby. I didn't know my wife had super-fast mood swings," He says, his hands placed on his hips.

"You learned something new about your wife. That's a good thing," I reply, my giggle still hanging in the air.

I shift around, trying to find some relief from the weight of my lehenga.

"You must be so uncomfortable in that. Let's switch to something more comfy," Samir suggests with a concerned tone in his voice.

I quickly nod. "You go ahead and change first. I'll take off all the jewelry. It'll take some time."

"Sure, my queen," hc replies right away.

I grab hold of my heavy lehenga, carefully slide off the bed, and make my way over to the dressing table to remove my accessories.

It's been a solid twenty minutes and I'm still struggling to get a hairpin that stubbornly lodged below my hairline. Since it's out of my sight, I can't figure out how it got stuck there.

The bathroom door opens with a light squeak, causing my eyes to drift over to Samir.

My heart skips a beat.

Drops of water trickle down his hair, caressing his nose, lips, and jaw. I watch him drying his hair with a towel and then our eyes meet.

"You wanna say something?" His voice startles me, instantly leaving me at a loss for words. "Umm... I-" I stumble.

His gaze intensifies, making it even harder for me to gather my thoughts. "I can't get the clips out of my hair, can you help me?" I blurt out.

His lips curve up into a smile. He tosses the towel onto the nearby couch and positions himself right behind me, his eyes carefully scanning my hair for that hairpin. And then his eyes come to a halt. "Found it" He says and with all his focus, he sets out to remove the pin from my hair.

I catch a glimpse of him in the mirror, and my heart melts at how adorable he looks when he's so focused. His lips press together, allowing his dimples to pop out.

These dimples are my weakness!

Without wasting a second, I reach for my phone on the dressing table and quietly open the camera before snapping some endearing pictures of him.

He's so focused on my hair that he doesn't even realize I've captured a memory of us together. "Done!" A wide smile graces his lips, causing me to smile back at him. "Thank you."

After I'm done with my night routine, I return to the bed and look over at Samir. He immediately gets up from the bed, clutching the back of his neck. "Ummm, you can take any side."

A chuckle escapes my lips. "It's alright... I'm okay with this side,"

As I lay on the bed, I inhale deeply, and gaze up at the ceiling, too nervous to meet his eyes. But finally I gather my courage and steal a glance at him. Yet, I quickly avert my gaze as I realize his eyes are already fixed upon me.

A brief silence envelops us, leaving us both searching for words.

"Do you have any secrets?" I ask, breaking the silence between us.

It is then that he shifts his body towards mine, his eyebrows knitting together. "No. I don't think so," he replies. "What about you?"

I mirror his movement, turning my entire body to face him, snuggled beneath the warm embrace of the cozy blanket. "Yes, I do have one"

"Really? I'm curious"

I take a deep breath and then finally speak, my voice betraying the fluttering butterflies in my stomach. "I've had a little crush on you even before we met in person," I confess.

His eyes widen. "Wait, you're serious?"

I smile. "Yes. Ever since I saw your pictures with Sara. And when I finally met you that day for the first time, I was completely smitten."

He inches closer to me, smiling ear to ear. "So... That means... It's..."

I don't let him finish as I say, "It's, she fell first."

He gently brushes his thumb against my cheek. "And he fell harder."

We share a chuckle together, and then, as our gazes meet, our smiles fade. His focus shifts to my lips. He gently rests his fingers over my cheeks and I can feel the warmth of his palm against my skin.

"You have no idea how long I have waited to make you mine. You have no idea how much I have yearned to hold you like this." he whispers. His heart thumps louder, and I can hear each beat clearly.

His lips immediately capture mine as he closes the distance between us. Our bodies press against each other. He kisses every inch of my lips, claiming them as his.

His touch sends a sudden shiver through my entire body as his hand slowly traces the curves of my figure, finally resting on my waist. With a firm grip, he pulls me even closer, deepening the kiss.

His lips, his breath, his weight pressing against me, I can feel it all, every inch of his presence, consuming me entirely.

TWENTY-SEVEN
ALEENA

The warm rays of sunlight caress my face, gently nudging me awake from my sleep. Slowly, I open my eyes, greeted by the most beautiful sight before me.

A smile tugs at the corners of my lips as I gaze at Samir's peaceful sleeping face. Starting my day with this adorable sight of him is seriously everything.

His eyes squint slightly as the sunlight hits his face. I lift my hand to block the light, hoping he can doze off again, but it's already too late.

His eyes open and catch me admiring him. An adorable smile graces his lips as he scrunches his eyes to get a better view. "Good morning, Love" he utters with his sleepy voice that melts my heart.

"Good Morning" I say and cup his cheeks. "Give me a smile" Instantly, his most adorable dimples appear, and I can't resist leaning in to place sweet kisses on them. We nestle together beneath the blanket, our bodies pressed close, and I can feel his laughter vibrating against me. "You seem so much into my dimples."

"Um, can we not talk about it?"

"No," he insists.

"Fine. I'll confess," I say with a smile. "Your dimples are my weakness."

His arms around me tighten, pulling me closer to him. He nuzzles his nose against my neck, hiding his face as his arms embrace me. Pressing deeper into my neck, he places a tender kiss, sending sudden shivers down my body.

I give his hair a gentle stroke, feeling its softness beneath my touch. "I gotta get up now and get ready." I whisper.

He nods in response but his face remains nestled against my neck, his arms refusing to release their loving grip. A giggle escapes my lips. "Come on. Otherwise, I'll end up running late." Eventually, he loosens his grip and his eyes meet mine.

I slide down the bed, reaching for my hair band to put my hair in a loose bun. "Don't tie it up, you look cute just like this," he says, catching my attention. I turn around to face him. "You think I'm cute like this?" I ask, pointing at my morning self. "You're perfect in every way. Nothing can change the fact how beautiful you are in my eyes, Aleena."

I feel like I have lost my ability to speak in front of him. His words pierces my heart, as if they are meant to stay there forever. The way he speaks those words, with love gleaming in his eyes, it truly means everything to me.

This man, every word he utters, every gaze he gives, has such a deep impact on me.

I swiftly turn away, rushing to the bathroom to conceal my flushed face.

I stand in front of the mirror, my eyes tracing every detail of the exquisite sari I'm wearing. The beautiful purple hue of the fabric gracefully dances under the warm glow of the lights.

And then, Samir emerges from the washroom, dressed in a soft blue shirt. He is looking absolutely perfect. His eyes lock onto me, causing me to smile. "How do I look?" I ask.

Closing the distance between us, he wraps his arms around me, planting a sweet, gentle kiss on my lips. "Beautiful as always," he whispers.

I giggle. "How do you always manage to melt my heart huh?"

He smirks. "Well, that's a secret"

"Fine, keep it under wraps. Now, let's head downstairs. Everyone must be waiting."

He nods in agreement.

Once we reach downstairs, I spot Sara, Mubashira Apu, Raisa Bhabi, Samir's parents, and others. Our eyes meet, and the room explodes with cheers and applause. Samir's mom walks up to me with a warm smile. "Oh, honey, you look so so beautiful in this sari!"

"After all, it was chosen by you." I reply, flashing her a smile. I make my way towards the others, "Aleena, you look so pretty, MashaAllah," Sara exclaims.

I smile at her in response.

"Aleena" Yasir calls out, causing me to shift my gaze towards him. However, before he can say anything further, Samir swiftly positions himself between us, a sardonic smile appears on his lips. "Bhabi. She's your bhabi now."

I press my lips together, doing my utmost to hold back the smile that's starting to appear on my face.

My Jealous Husband is back.

"Alright, bro! Cool down. I'll call her bhabi," Yasir chuckles, tapping Samir's arm lightly. As Samir glances back at me, I can't hold myself anymore and end up laughing.

"Why are you laughing?" he asks. I'm just about to reply when Raisa bhabi pulls me aside.

"Come here, you can talk to him later. We've got some serious fun to have," Mubashira apu says from behind. I walk over to them with Raisa bhabi by my side.

NEXT DAY

I stumble wearily into my bedroom, my body craving the comfort of my bed. With a heavy sigh, I let myself collapse onto the soft mattress, feeling the weight of exhaustion dragging me down.

"Tired?" Samir asks, and I simply nod. "Yeah, a bit. Ma insisted I take some rest before heading to the beauty parlour for our walima."

My way of addressing Samir's mom has changed from 'Aunty' to 'Ma.'

A gentle smile graces Samir's face as he draws nearer, his hand reaching out to gently ruffle my hair. "Why don't you take a nap?" he suggests.

But I shake my head immediately. "No, if I give in to sleep now, even for a short while, I know I'll wake up with a pounding headache or in a foul mood. Nah, I'd rather stay awake."

He chuckles. "Okay, then just take it easy. I need to discuss a few things with Sahil bhaiya. I'll go find him."

I nod in response. "Okay,"

And then makes his way out of the room.

I reach for my phone, hoping to keep myself awake with some scrolling. I mindlessly scroll through all the notifications and updates and the weariness that has plagued me begins to take its toll. The weight of exhaustion settles upon my eyelids, and before I realize it, I have drifted off into a deep sleep.

"Aleena, Aleena," Samir's voice gently caresses my ears, and it's enough to rouse me from my sleep.

"You said you wouldn't sleep, but you ended up dozing off," he laughs.

I blink away the remnants of drowsiness and glance at my phone, still clutched in my hand. "Uff! I accidentally fell asleep."

Samir chuckles, gets up on the bed and then his lips curve into a smirk. "So, should I help you stay awake?" he teases. I laugh and push him away. "Don't start teasing me now."

"Why not?" he whispers, inching closer to me.

"Shut up" I response, giggling.

"But, you haven't even heard of the plan yet. What are you thinking?" He smirks.

THIS MAN!

"Okay. What's your plan then?"

Before I can even process his response, he starts tickling me. "Samir, stop! It's tickling!" I manage to say in between fits of laughter. But he doesn't let up, continuing to tickle me while laughing along. I try to push him away, but our struggle ends with him lying on the bed and me on top of him. And still, he doesn't stop, tickling me while my hair cascades over his face.

I manage to slip away from his grasp and slide down the bed. "Samir, I'm telling you, stop!" I exclaim, darting around the room as he chases after me.

In a swift motion, I snatch a pillow from the bed and hurl it towards him, but he skillfully dodges it. "You can't get me that easily with this pillow, wifey! Now come here to me!" he says, giggling uncontrollably with me.

"Samir, I'm telling you for the last time, knock it off!"

"Nah,"

"You better listen."

"Oh, come on, don't be shy, wifey. Come over here."

"Shy? Seriously? My stomach hurts from laughing too much, and it's all because of you."

"Haha let me make you laugh even more"

"No, Samir Zafar"

"Yes, Aleena Noor"

"Nooooooo"

"Yesssssss"

TWENTY-EIGHT
ALEENA

As we stroll into the beautifully decorated lawn, a rush of memories floods in. It's crazy to think that just yesterday we were celebrating our walima. And now, here we are, back home after seeing my parents off at the airport.

As Sara spots us, she calls out, "Here comes our new couple! Come on, sit with us." Her warm smile instantly puts me at ease. Sahil bhaiya, Raisa bhabi, Eshan bhaiya, Mubashira apu, and all our other cousins are here too. I walk up to hold Raisa Bhabi's adorable baby in my arms. She had been blessed with twins merely a year ago.

"So Samir bhaiya's wedding functions are over too. I'm gonna miss every memory we made together," Sara says and a chorus of agreements follows.

"Isn't it incredible? I mean, who could have possibly foreseen this would happen? We all came here together for Sahil's wedding, and who knew that another unexpected match would come out of it." Mubashira Apu exclaims, her eyes shifting between me and Samir.

"Well, I gotta admit, it was unexpected for me as well." I reply, my gaze meeting Samir's as he flashes a smile.

"By the way, how's our newlywed couple's day going?" Mubashira Apu suddenly asks, grabbing our attention. "That's a secret, I ain't spillin' the beans," Samir playfully retorts, prompting a chuckle to escape from my lips.

"Okay, if you are not spilling this secret, how about sharing any other secrets, huh?" Raisa bhabi asks. At her question, Samir and I look at each other, our eyes telling each other exactly what we want to share with everyone. And then we look back at them.

"There is one," Samir says and I smile, knowing exactly what he's about to say. We can feel the intense curiosity from everyone. "Aleena and I actually started liking each other way before our parents arranged our marriage."

To our surprise, everyone falls into an awkward silence. Confusion floods over both Samir and me as we exchange puzzled glances, wondering why there's no reaction. But then, Sara pipes up, "Act surprised, act surprised!" She nudges Mubashira apu, and they both start acting all shocked. It's as if they've been in on our little secret all along.

"Wait, hold up! Did you all already know?" I ask and everyone erupts into laughter.

"Well, you better ask your husband about that one," Sara says. "And, let me take some more credits. Remember that day when the two of you were fighting over that picture?"

~

"Samir, delete the picture!"

Aleena continues her relentless pursuit to snatch the phone from Samir. Sara and her mother observe the scene silently. "They are looking cute together," Sara's mom giggles, enjoying the sight before her.

"Exactly, Mom! They look cute TOGETHER!" Sara emphasizes the word 'together,' hoping her mom catches on

to something. Abruptly, her mom's eyes widen. "'Why didn't I think of this before?"

"It's alright, Mom! But you get it now, right?" Sara asks.

"Absolutely!" her mom replies, stealing another glance at Aleena and Samir. "So, go talk to Dad about it! And drop some hints to Aleena's parents too, okay?" Sara suggests, prompting her mom to nod in agreement.

As she is about to leave the room, she looks back at Aleena and Samir and secretly captures a picture of them. With a wide smile, she quietly exits the room, with Sara trailing behind.

~

I look over at Samir, my eyes widening in surprise.

He shrugs. "I didn't know about it, trust me! And I also didn't expect everyone else to find out,"

"Remember that day when you said, 'My future wife doesn't count as anyone'? We were all awake at that time. That's when I found out, and I confirmed it with Sara," Mubashira apu explains, making my eyes widen even more.

"And the rest of us found out later from Sara and Mubashira apu," Sahil bhaiya adds.

I cover my mouth in shock, still processing everything. "Seriously, guys? I feel so betrayed now,"

I look back at Samir and in the next moment we burst into laughter together, realizing that our little secret wasn't so secret after all.

TWENTY-NINE
ALEENA

Samir is busy with Sahil bhaiya and Sara is engrossed in an online meeting regarding her studies, and here I am, strolling up to the rooftop. I step further until I reach the edge of the roof. I lean against the sturdy railing, taking in the breathtaking view before me. The cool night breeze gently brushes against my face, giving me a slight chill.

"Hey!"

I jump slightly and look next to me. "Samir!"

"You scared me! When did you come?"

He smiles, showing his adorable dimples. "Just now. I saw you coming here"

"So you're following me" I quip.

He places his elbows over the railing, leaning his back against it. "Well, I remember someone telling me to follow my heart. So I'm just going with the flow"

"That someone thought you were tangled in other stuff, but that someone didn't realize that the something you were stressed with was actually all about that someone you deeply fell in love with." I blurt out the words and he starts chuckling. "Is that some kind of tongue twister?"

"Sort of" I reply, giggling along.

"The henna looks so pretty on your hands," he says, gently taking my hand that still bears the intricate patterns from our Mehedi ceremony.

I smile. "I've always loved wearing henna."

"Really?" he asks.

"Yup! When I was a kid, I used to apply henna a lot. My grandma had a henna tree, so she would collect the henna leaves, make a paste, and apply it on my hands. I remember she used to make this huge circle on my palm with henna and also cover my fingertips with it. Sometimes, I would even try to apply the henna myself, but I would always end up creating weird shapes instead of perfect circles." I finish my words with a giggle.

"Then you should apply it more often," he says.

"There's a secret, I still have no idea how to do it!" I whisper.

"Don't worry, I'll learn for you and apply henna on your hand myself," he replies, smiling.

"No way, you're seriously going to learn?"

"For you? Yes,"

Okay someone needs to stop this man, my heart can't handle it anymore!

Soon a silence stretches between us. The moon is shining bright, casting its glow over the rooftop. We stand side by side, bathed in the soft glow. I keep my eyes focused on the sky above, but I can sense Samir's gaze on me. I steal a quick glance in his direction. "What are you looking at?"

A gentle smile tucks on his lips. "What do you think I'm looking at?" I bob my head, turning and mirroring his position. "Maybe the beautiful lady standing next to you"

His dimples appear once again. "I gotta admit, the lady next to me is actually pretty."

"But my wife is prettier," he adds.

I raise my eyebrows, grinning from ear to ear. "Really? How pretty?"

His gaze lingers on me for a moment, and I patiently wait for him to say the words. "She's so breathtakingly beautiful that whenever I lay my eyes on her, I lose all my power to look away."

I smile, this time even wider. "Seems like she's really so beautiful."

"No doubts about it," he chuckles.

"You love her so much?" I ask, my heart pounding in my chest.

"Obviously" he replies, no hesitation whatsoever.

My chest fills with warmth.

My stomach flutters with butterflies.

And chills run down my entire body.

Each time his words of love caress my ears, it evokes the same special feeling that I crave, over and over again.

"How much do you love her?"

His eyes narrow playfully. "Why should I tell you?"

"You love teasing, don't you?" I ask, giggling.

He takes a step closer. "With you? Yes"

His hand brushes through my hair, sweeping them off my shoulder, allowing them to cascade down my back.

"Give me a smile," I whisper, and this time, his eyes meet mine once again. "Why?" A chuckle escapes his lips, making his dimples to shine like two adorable little dancers on his cheeks.

I tiptoe, reaching up to his cheeks, and gently rest my hands behind his ears.

I shower his dimples with kisses.

I find my balance again, and as I glance up, his smile disappears from his face. He moves closer, standing right in front of me, his body facing mine. Taking another step, he places his hands on either side of me on the railing, enclosing me within his arms.

With a gentle touch, I trace my finger over his dimples, feeling his body respond to each and every one of my tender caresses.

"I love you" I whisper softly. And this time I see his chest rising and falling even faster.

He leans in, placing a kiss at the corner of my lips, reigniting the fluttering butterflies in my stomach. Slowly, he moves to the other corner, leaving a gentle kiss there. He slowly traces his lips along my jawline, leaving a trail of kisses that send shivers down my body. Finally his lips return to mine.

He kisses me.

The air crackles with tension as he leans in further, his lips meeting mine in a gentle yet firm kiss, a delicate dance between passion and restraint.

THIRTY
SAMIR

I walk into my room and spot my mom sitting on the bed, right in front of Aleena, coaxing her to eat the fruits on the plate. "Aleena, you have to eat these fruits, dear. Don't be stubborn,"

Aleena shakes her head. Her eyes squint ever so slightly, and she tilts her head back a little, clearly showing her disinterest. "I really don't want to eat, Ma."

My mom constantly tries to persuade Aleena to eat the fruits, but she remains steadfast in her refusal. After a little back-and-forth she eventually gives in reluctantly.

I watch my mom feeding Aleena the fruits with utmost care and tenderness. Then, she turns to me with a proud smile. "Look, finally I made your wife eat these fruits. You couldn't even do that,"

I take a glance at Aleena and in the next moment she erupts into giggles.

"I have to go now. Aleena, dear, take rest." Planting a gentle kiss on Aleena's forehead, my mom leaves the room.

I turn my gaze towards Aleena. Taking a step closer, I reach out to gently touch her hair. "How are you feeling now?"

A smile brightens her face. "Better."

I scoot closer to her and caress her beautiful baby bump, feeling the little one within. Looking up at her, I gently cup her cheeks and press my lips on hers.

"I can't wait to hold our child in my arms," I whisper. She smiles, mirroring the happiness in mine.

I feel a little shake on my arms, causing me to jolt out of my sleep. "Aleena! What happened? What happened?" I ask all worried, realizing it's her who woke me up.

"Calm down, calm down, I'm okay," she assures, gently cupping my cheeks. I shift my gaze towards the window but the curtain blocks my view, preventing me from seeing clearly. But through the tiny gap in the curtains, I peer outside and notice that the sky is dimly lit, indicating that dawn is approaching, the sun hasn't risen yet.

"What's the matter?" I whisper.

"Umm... I can't sleep." she replies.

I gently place my palm over her cheeks. "Why love?"

"Calm down, it's just that I woke up from sleep out of nowhere and now I don't feel sleepy anymore."

"Come here, I'll help you fall asleep," I stretch out my arms but she shakes her head, refusing my offer. "I don't want to sleep"

I raise an eyebrow, silently asking what she has in mind. She gazes out the window, lost in thought for a moment and then, with a grin, she turns to me. "Let's go watch the sunrise."

I glance at the clock on my bedside table and then look back at her. "Right now? That's so sudden"

"Please, let's go. We still have time to reach the spot before the sun rises," she urges me.

I slowly rub my eyes, trying to shake off the last remnants of sleep, and then I turn my gaze back to her. "Alright. Let's get ready."

"So we are going?"

"Yes"

She squirms beneath the blanket and plants a quick kiss on my lips. "Thank you!"

We quickly freshen up and get dressed before heading out to our destination. We decided not to disturb our family members, as we will only be away for an hour.

And we can share about it once they wake up.

After helping Aleena out of the car, I grip her hand tightly and we stroll ahead, gazing up at the sky. The air feels crisp, bringing a different calmness that surrounds us. We stand there, taking in the incredible beauty of nature.

The sun continues its ascent, casting its golden glow upon us. I steal a glance at Aleena. Her eyes are sparkling with joy.

Suddenly, a rush of memories floods my mind.

It's that day—the day I witnessed the sunrise with her for the first time.

The day, I realized she was the one I wanted by my side for the rest of my life.

Every single detail of that day keeps flashing through my mind, bringing a wide grin to my face.

And now, she's my wife, carrying our precious child in her womb. It still feels like a dream....an enchanting dream.

Leaning in, I gently press a kiss on the side of her forehead. "Do I annoy you a lot?" she unexpectedly asks, a tinge of sadness in her expression. I gently shake my head and turn her to face me completely.

"Not at all, my love," I whisper. "You are carrying our child within you, enduring the pain of motherhood alone. I am just trying my best to take care of both my babies. Compared to your incredible strength as a mother, my efforts are nothing. You have never annoyed me Aleena, not for a single moment."

Her eyes shimmer with tears and a smile graces her lips. "I love you a lot, Samir," she whispers, filling my heart with warmth. I gently brush away her tears, preventing them from tracing her beautiful cheeks, and place a gentle kiss on her forehead.

"I love you more Aleena. My love for you blooms with every heartbeat, every breath, every fleeting second. I love you. I love you so much more, my queen. Even More than the word LOVE can express"

Epilogue

ALEENA

<u>**YEAR-2024**</u>
<u>*Florida, US*</u>

"Do you think she will have dimples like you?" I murmur, my gaze fixed on our daughter as Samir lies beside her.

A chuckle escapes his throat. "You're always obsessed with dimples,"

I smile. "Yes, I am."

He reaches out to cradle our daughter in his arms, his hands gently securing her. "She's so pretty, MashaAllah," he whispers and then steals a glance at me. "Just like her mom."

I let out a soft chuckle, my eyes shifting to him. But then I catch a glimpse of our daughter, her adorable round eyes fixated on her father. "Aleesa," I softly call out, but her gaze remains locked on him. "Seems like she really enjoyed your sweet praises."

Samir locks his gazes with Aleesa, smiling at her. Just then, a sudden phone call interrupts us, drawing my attention to the screen. With a quick swipe, I see that it's Dad calling. "Oh, it's Baba. Perhaps the surprise went well," I exclaim, answering the call.

Dad had flown to New York earlier to surprise Sara and he planned to spend the night there. Since it's just a 2 and a half hour flight from Florida to New York, we didn't have to worry too much about it.

"Assalamu Alaikum, Baba," I greet him, and Samir does the same. I can see Sara sitting next to him, her eyes glued to us. "Walaikum Assalam," Dad replies, his smile reaching his eyes. "Hi Sara!" I say excitedly, and soon a wide smile graces her face in return.

"Hi!" she responds, while Samir waves at her too. "What's our little Aleesa doing?" Dad asks. I turn the camera to capture our daughter, only to find her peacefully asleep in Samir's arms.

"Dad, how's everything going over there?" Samir inquires.

A twinkle of excitement dances in Dad's eyes as a broad smile spreads across his face. "We just finished our dinner now. And let me tell you, I had an absolutely fantastic day"

Samir gently puts Aleesa's sleeping figure back on the bed and then he gets all focused on his phone screen. "Oh really?"

"Yes, actually, Aryan was with me. And he's the one who prepared the entire meal for us today. He's such a nice guy." Dad steals a quick glance at Sara, and I notice a subtle change in her expression after hearing Aryan's name.

"Aryan?" I inquire.

"Yes, I told you about him before. Remember Habib? Sara's patient? Aryan is his son. What a perfect young man he is!" Dad exclaims and I can hear Samir chuckling next to me.

Sara lets out a sigh, almost as if she's not interested in discussing him right now or perhaps she would rather not bring it up in this conversation at all. "Okay, Dad, how much more are you going to praise him?"

I realize that he is the person dad has mentioned to us several times before, and I have a feeling that Dad's surprise visit to New York had a little something to do with meeting him too.

I give Sara a glance through the screen and then turn my attention back to Dad, feeling an urge to tease her a bit because I can already sense what's coming next.

"Baba, what was his name again?"

"Aryan. Aryan Kabir"

END

About The Author

Noor, an author from Bangladesh who is an introvert but completely an opposite person whenever she is around the people close to her. The Unexpected Match is her first-ever project. Through this story she highlighted the beauty of Bangladeshi culture to the world and emphasized the importance of family and their love.

Translations

Ma - Mom
Baba - Dad
Bhaiya - Elder Brother
Apu - Elder sister
Bhabi - Sisters-in-law
Chachi - Aunt
Khala - Aunt